Andrea Carter's

Tales *from the*
Circle C Ranch

Also by Susan K. Marlow

Circle C Beginnings
Andi's Pony Trouble
Andi's Indian Summer
Andi's Scary School Days
Andi's Fair Surprise
Andi's Lonely Little Foal
Andi's Circle C Christmas

Circle C Adventures
Andrea Carter and the Long Ride Home
Andrea Carter and the Dangerous Decision
Andrea Carter and the Family Secret
Andrea Carter and the San Francisco Smugglers
Andrea Carter and the Trouble with Treasure
Andrea Carter and the Price of Truth

Circle C Milestones
Thick as Thieves
Heartbreak Trail

Goldtown Adventures
Badge of Honor
Tunnel of Gold
Canyon of Danger
River of Peril

Andrea Carter's
Tales *from the*
Circle C Ranch

Susan K. Marlow

Kregel
Publications

Andrea Carter's Tales from the Circle C Ranch
© 2015 by Susan K. Marlow

Cover, "Britches Are Not for Little Girls," and "Aunt Rebecca
and the Hat" illustrations © 2015 by Leslie Gammelgaard

All other illustrations © 2015 by Melissa McConnell

Published by Kregel Publications, a division of Kregel, Inc.,
2450 Oak Industrial Dr. NE, Grand Rapids, MI 49505.

ISBN 978-0-8254-4379-4

Printed in the United States of America
15 16 17 18 19 / 5 4 3 2 1

Contents

Part I

The Early Years

I

Britches Are Not for Little Girls

September 1873
This story takes place the autumn before Andi's Pony Trouble.

"LITTLE GIRLS DO *not* wear britches."

Mother didn't raise her voice, but she sounded firm. Like always.

I peeked around my ten-year-old sister, Melinda, and looked down the long table. Father sat at the head of the table, sipping a cup of after-supper coffee.

He didn't say anything right away. He put down his coffee cup and scooped up a piping hot forkful of apple pie, fresh from the oven.

"First of the season, *Señor* Carter," Luisa told him as she cleared away the dirty dishes.

"It's delicious," Father said.

Luisa beamed. *"Muchas gracias, señor."*

Father was the tallest and strongest man in the whole world. Dressed in his fancy dinner clothes, he was also the most handsome.

Our family always dressed for the evening meal. It was *The Rule*. Even my two oldest brothers, who were grown up, didn't come to the table in work clothes.

Chad tried to once. He burst into the house with a story about the cattle herd that Mother and Father listened to with interest. Before we knew it, the supper bell was ringing. Father led Mother toward the dining room.

"I assume, Chad, that you will be dining with us this evening?" Mother said over her shoulder.

You never saw a twenty-year-old race so fast upstairs to change!

I didn't like dressing up for dinner . . . or for anything else. Play dresses with aprons were good enough for me. Most days I ran out of the house barefoot. I'd be off playing with the ranch hands' children before Mother could catch me.

Right now, I was watching Father eat his pie. Would he answer Mother?

I sighed. The "britches" subject was my own fault, and my new friend Riley's idea. He had just come to live on our ranch with his Uncle Sid, the ranch foreman. Chad told me Riley's mother was sick, and his father was an army captain often away on patrol. Riley would be staying on the ranch until his mother was well.

We took to each other right away.

When I had trouble getting up on his big, black horse, Riley said, "You can't do it in a dress, Andi. Even if you make it, your skirt will get all scrunched up. Your bloomers will get dirty, and your bare legs will show. I bet your mama wouldn't like that."

Riley was right. Mother would not like that at all.

I followed Riley into the room he shared with his Uncle Sid just behind the bunkhouse. He dug around in an orange crate and pulled out a pair of overalls.

"I'm a cowboy now," he said, "so I'm gonna dress like one, in britches and a shirt. You can have my overalls."

I squealed my joy. "Thank you, Riley!"

Overalls were the answer to all my riding problems, if only Mother and Father would agree.

Every day while Melinda was away at school, Father tossed me up on Caesar, his big, bay horse. Father let me go everywhere with him, sitting on his lap in the saddle. He rode out to the herd, gave orders to the cowhands, and taught Chad and Mitch how to run the ranch. Sometimes I asked questions, but most of the time I just watched everything from high up on Caesar's broad back.

The only dark cloud rose when the town ladies showed up on the ranch to visit Mother. They clucked their tongues and said it was not proper for a little girl to ride astride, with her skirts flying and her knees showing.

"It's downright shameful, Elizabeth," Mrs. Peterson told Mother. "You ought to put a stop to it."

Father disagreed. "The child loves to ride, and she's a born horsewoman. Only the livestock, her brothers, and a few old cowhands see Andrea's skirts flying." When the ladies left, he frowned. "I see no reason to pay any attention to busybodies."

"Busybodies are folks who mind everybody's business but their own," Chad said when I asked him what the word meant.

Father and Mother did not pay busybodies any mind . . . except for one.

Aunt Rebecca, the busiest busybody of all, nearly fainted when she saw Father and me on Caesar one day during a surprise visit. She scolded Father something fierce, but he just laughed.

"This is a very serious matter, James," Aunt Rebecca said, frowning.

Father stopped laughing. "If it bothers you that much, dear

sister, all right." Then he handed me down to Aunt Rebecca and put Caesar away. I didn't go riding again with Father until Aunt Rebecca went home to San Francisco.

Yes, overalls were the answer to all my problems. I was sure of it.

◆ ◆ ◆

All those memories were swirling around inside my head while Father ate his pie and the boys talked about dull, grown-up things.

I looked at Justin, my oldest brother. He had been home only a couple of months since graduating from law school. I felt a little funny around him. He'd been away at college for three years. I didn't know him very well. Holidays were too short to get to know somebody, even your own big brother.

Justin saw me looking at him and leaned across the table. "I'll take you riding after supper if you like," he whispered.

I nodded. Then I looked at Father. He was still eating his pie. It was a big piece.

He caught my gaze and winked.

Father's wink made me feel warm and cozy all over. It meant he had everything under control—even a mealtime discussion about the proper dress for little girls on a ranch.

"A pair of overalls is the only practical solution, Elizabeth," Father said. "Andrea's little frocks would stay cleaner that way." He smiled.

I forgot about Justin's offer of an after-supper horseback ride. This was important. I put my fork down and sat perfectly still.

"Jim," Mother said, frowning. "It's unseemly. Little girls do not wear britches . . . or overalls."

I ducked my head. Maybe I shouldn't have come to lunch

today in Riley's overalls. I should have taken them off and kept them in the orange crate—just Riley's and my secret.

"Who in the world makes these rules?" Father wanted to know. It was not a question he expected an answer to.

I answered anyway. "Aunt Rebecca."

Everyone burst out laughing. I grinned and laughed too, but I didn't know why. It really wasn't funny. Aunt Rebecca thought up all the rules that made me miserable.

Father winked at me again. "If it were only that simple, sweetheart." He turned to Mother. "Skirts and horses do not mix, dear. Did you take one of Melinda's frocks, split the front and back, and sew it up for leggings like I asked?"

Mother nodded.

"It works just dandy, Father," Melinda said. "My split skirt stays where I want it to when I go riding."

Father grunted and looked pleased.

"You could teach the girls to ride sidesaddle," Mother said.

Sidesaddle? What's that? I wondered.

Father frowned, and his eyes flashed blue fire. "My dear, I want *all* of our children to be safe, not just the boys. Riding sidesaddle is an outlandish, dangerous way for a young lady to ride a horse."

"Who made *that* rule?" I couldn't help asking. "That ladies have to ride that way?" I still didn't know what "sidesaddle" was.

Nobody got after me for speaking without being spoken to.

"Who knows?" Justin said. "It's not a law. Just one of those things society expects of ladies."

Father frowned. "We are three thousand miles away from the East. I won't let somebody's fool notion of what is or is not proper put my little girls in danger."

"San Francisco is only two hundred miles away," Justin put in.

"Let San Francisco take care of itself," Father said. "This is my ranch and my family. I think we can decide for ourselves how to live on it."

This sounded like good news to me. But I wasn't sure how the overalls came into it. I almost asked, but Father spoke again.

"I won't have a sidesaddle on this spread," he said. "The way Andrea rides, she'd break her neck riding that way." He shook his head. "No."

"All right, Jim," Mother said at last. "Shall I split Andrea's dresses? I might as well do them all. She'll go through them quickly enough."

I knew I was hard on clothes. *I would rather have overalls*, I pleaded silently. *Please, please, please!*

"Overalls are durable," Father said. "I see no harm in letting her wear them when she's with me, or when she rides Coco."

"She'll be in them every day then," Melinda piped up. "Just like a little tomboy." She looked at me and made a face. "*Tomboy*," she whispered in my ear.

"Melinda, that will do," Father said.

"Yes, sir." Melinda went back to her apple pie.

"So long as she understands they are only for riding here on the ranch," Mother said. "Andrea will not step a foot off this spread in overalls or britches. Is that understood?"

"Of course, dear," Father said. He smiled at me. "Andrea,

you heard your mother. You may wear overalls to ride, but you will not complain when it's time to change for supper or for going to town."

"Yes, Father," I said. Inside, I was jumping up and down.

I leaped from my chair and ran around the table to hug Father tight. I hugged Mother too. She didn't look quite as happy as Father.

"Can I keep the overalls in my wardrobe instead of in Riley's orange crate?" I asked, nearly out of breath.

"*May* I," Mother reminded me, but she nodded.

"Yippee!" I tore out of the dining room. From behind I heard Father laughing his big, deep laugh.

◆ ◆ ◆

When Father was thrown from his horse and killed the following spring, I refused to take off my overalls. I cried and cried and kept them on, no matter what anybody said. My overalls made me think of Father, and I did not want to forget him.

Every time I wore my overalls I smelled the slight odor of horses and sweet hay; I remembered Father's tickly beard on the back of my neck when I rode in front of him and he kissed the top of my head.

Those overalls—and Justin—helped me accept the fact that Father had gone to heaven and was not coming back.

Mother let me wear overalls for many years. When I outgrew the pair Riley gave me, I wore my brother Mitch's hand-me-downs. I think Mother knew it was one way I could keep Father close to my heart.

Britches might not be for little girls . . . but overalls are.

2

The Best Gift of All

October 1874
This story takes place during Andi's Scary School Days.

STANDING ON TIPTOE, I pressed my nose against the glass case in Mr. Goodwin's mercantile. So many pretty necklaces! So many rings and brooches! Which one would Mother like for her birthday? I clutched one dime and two pennies in my sweaty hand and tried to decide.

"How much is that one?" I pointed to a glittery, blue-glass brooch that would look lovely on Mother's Sunday best.

Mr. Goodwin smiled. "It's two—"

My heart soared in hope. *I can buy it!*

". . . dollars and twenty-five cents," Mr. Goodwin finished.

Just as quickly, my heart plunged to my toes. I had been going to school for only one month, so I didn't know much about arithmetic yet. But even *I* knew that two pennies and two dollars were miles apart. *And a dime is only ten cents*. No help there.

"Your mother would love it."

"No, thank you, sir. I'll keep looking."

I sighed and walked down the length of the glass case. Handkerchiefs? No. Wooden spoons? No. Hair pins? No. A mustache cup? Absolutely no! So many choices. But not many that two pennies and one dime would buy.

At the other end of the store my sister Melinda chatted with a friend from school. A little bug of jealousy pinched my thoughts.

It's not fair! Melinda knows exactly what she plans to buy. Melinda had saved her money for weeks to buy a soft, cozy, pink shawl Mother would love.

It wasn't that I had forgotten Mother's birthday. Not exactly. But weeks were so long, and things happened so fast (or so slow) that I had forgotten to save the pennies Mother or Justin gave me for chores or "just because."

It didn't help that I sometimes forgot to do my chores. On those days I didn't get any pennies. It also didn't help that I'd spent a lot of pennies on licorice whips and lemon drops.

"What did you buy?" Melinda came to stand beside me after saying good-bye to her friend.

"Nothing."

"What? You *have* to buy Mother a birthday gift. Think of all the nice things she does for you. She's never forgotten *your* birthday."

That was true, but when Melinda talked like she knew everything, it always got my "dander up," as Mitch sometimes said. I scowled. "I didn't forget. I'm going to buy her a present."

"What?"

"I'm still looking."

Melinda tapped her foot impatiently. "You'd better hurry. Justin will be by to pick us up in a few minutes."

"Is an hour up already?" How could time go by so fast? "Please help me, Melinda. What can I buy with my money?"

My sister sighed and shifted the brown paper package under her arm. "How much do you have?"

Opening my hand, I showed Melinda the dime and two pennies lying in my palm.

"Is that all? You can't buy anything for twelve cents."

If twelve cents could not buy Mother a nice gift, what would I do? It would be a horrible, terrible tragedy.

Everyone else had a nice gift for her. Melinda had the beautiful shawl. Justin had shown me a pretty pearl necklace he'd bought in San Francisco. Mitch and Chad had put their heads together and thought of something Mother would love—a new saddle.

But I won't have anything to give her.

I wanted to sit down on the wooden floor and cry. I remembered just in time that I was six years old and too big to act like a baby in the mercantile. So I pressed my lips together like Chad told me to do when I got hurt and needed to be brave.

I swallowed the lump in my throat. "Can't I buy *anything* with a dime and two pennies?"

Melinda shrugged. "Not anything nice. Maybe a few hair pins or a mouse trap."

A wrinkled my nose. A mouse trap? Why would Mother want a mouse trap?

"I suppose I could give you two quarters," Melinda said in a kinder voice. "That way you can get Mother a nice scarf or maybe a hairbrush."

I thought for a minute then said, "No. If you give me the money, then it isn't my present to Mother."

"Yes, it is."

I shook my head. It was hard to explain, especially to my big sister, but in my heart I knew a present should be something I bought myself, with my own money.

Melinda had saved her money; probably the rest of the family had too. It didn't seem right to take Melinda's money to buy a present from *me*.

Melinda let out a breath. "Here comes Justin. Let's see what he says."

"Well, lovely ladies, are you ready to go home?" Justin gave one of my dark braids a gentle tug. "What did you buy for Mother?"

"I bought her a new shawl," Melinda said before I could say one word. "But Andi didn't buy anything. She doesn't have enough money. I offered to give her some of mine, but she won't take it. Isn't that the silliest—"

"I want to buy a present for Mother my own self," I burst out. "With my *own* money."

I quickly ducked my head. Interrupting others, even a bossy big sister, was not polite. I waited for Justin to scold me.

He didn't. To my surprise, he squatted down until his blue eyes could look right into mine. "Why don't you tell me about it," he said in his calm, quiet voice.

"I already told you," Melinda said. "She only—"

"Melinda, perhaps you should wait in the buggy." Justin used his do-it-now voice. "I'll help Andi with her present."

I could tell Melinda didn't want to obey Justin. She scowled at me and flounced out of the store.

Things went much better after Melinda left. Justin let me look around while he made suggestions. But even Justin couldn't do much with twelve cents.

"Perhaps Mother would like lemon drops," he said. "You know she has a sweet tooth. Candy would be a nice birthday treat. You can buy a little sack of lemon drops for a dime."

"Luisa is making her a birthday cake," I said. "With white icing."

"Hmmm," Justin said thoughtfully. "I see."

Pretty soon, I was feeling a little desperate. The same way I felt when Chad told me to do a chore and I dawdled too long. *I have to hurry up and find something*, I told myself, *or Mother's birthday will come and I won't be ready.*

"I have an idea," Justin said when I felt a few tears leaking out. "Why don't you draw Mother a picture? She loved the picture you drew last week of Coco. A drawing wouldn't cost anything."

I twirled the end of my braid and shrugged. "It doesn't seem as special as a shawl or a saddle or a pearl necklace."

"It would be special if it was in this beautiful frame," Mr. Goodwin said from behind the counter. He held up a small, gold-gilded frame that would look beautiful on top of Mother's dresser.

I caught my breath. A perfect present! "Does it cost a dime and two pennies?"

"Well," Mr. Goodwin said, "I'm afraid not."

My heart went flip-flop. *Not again!*

Then Justin made it all better. "You know what, Andi? This frame does cost more than twelve cents, but I'll make a deal with—"

"If you give me the money, it won't be my present," I said.

Justin laughed and tweaked my other braid. "Honey, I wouldn't dream of giving you the money. But if you promise to work for it, I could see my way clear to making you a small loan. You could pay me back later."

"I could?" This sounded too good to be true. "And it would still be all from me?"

Justin nodded. "You'd be paying for it, but *after* you buy it."

I knew from seeing Justin's and Mr. Goodwin's smiles that this was going to work. The beautiful frame would be perfect.

I handed over my dime and two pennies, and Mr. Goodwin wrapped the frame in brown paper. I couldn't see how much Justin gave the storekeeper, but a minute later he took out a little book from his inside vest pocket and wrote something down.

"I'm recording how much you owe me in extra chores, so we don't forget," Justin explained before I could ask. He frowned at me, but it was not a for-real frown. "You had better not skip town before you do the work, either." Then he winked. "I know where you live."

I giggled.

Hugging the package to the front of my dress, I walked with Justin to the buggy. He lifted me in beside Melinda and then went around to get in on the other side.

"What did you buy?" Melinda asked. "Did Justin give you the money?"

"I'm doing extra chores for the money," I told her. "Justin wrote down exactly how much I have to pay him back."

"Oh, for pity's sake—"

Justin cleared his throat, and Melinda closed her mouth.

It was so close to suppertime when we got home that I panicked. Here was this beautiful frame but there was no drawing in it! There wasn't time to draw another picture of Coco. That one had taken me almost an hour to draw.

What am I going to do?

When I have to, I can think fast. I thought fast right then. I grabbed a sheet of paper from Justin's desk and a pencil. Running up to the room I shared with Melinda, I sat down on the floor and thought.

What can I draw? For practice, I traced around one of my hands. Then I got an idea.

"Andi, it's time to get ready for supper." Melinda came into the room with a pitcher of clean water. "What are you doing? What kind of drawing is that?" She bent over my shoulder.

"It's my handprint, with little hearts all around it," I answered. I'd found some crayons and colored the hearts red and pink. I looked up. "Melinda, can you please write the words for me? I'll tell you what to say."

Sometimes Melinda could be very nice. She set down the pitcher and said, "Sure. What do you want me to write?"

"Dear Mother," I began.

Melinda formed the letters in her best penmanship. "Got that," she said. "Now what?"

"I drew my left hand, the one closest to my heart. Love, Andi."

Melinda finished writing then handed me the pencil. "You know how to write your own name. You can do that part."

I took the pencil and did my best, but it didn't look very good. Worse, Melinda had a puzzled expression on her face. "What does it mean, anyway?" she asked.

My stomach turned over. It was a beautiful frame, but what if Mother didn't understand the words either?

"Remember when Mother was teaching me what hand was my left hand and what hand was my right hand?"

Melinda nodded.

"She asked me to tell her what hand Mitch used to hold the reins, or what hand Justin used to write with, or what hand Luisa used to stir the soup. Remember?"

"I said I remembered. So, why did you draw your *left* hand?"

"Well . . ." I swallowed. Father had died last spring, two months before I turned six. I didn't have very many memories of him. Not nearly as many as Melinda or Mitch had, or especially not as many memories as Justin or Chad or Mother.

"Well, *what*?" Melinda said.

It was my own special memory. But maybe if I told Melinda, she wouldn't laugh. Maybe she would understand what my drawing meant.

"Father always patted my head with his left hand," I said. "And he tugged on my braid with the same hand. One day, I asked him why he always used his *left* hand. He told me it's because it was the hand closest to his heart, and it had the most love, and . . ."

I felt a tear come. I couldn't say any more.

Melinda reached out and squeezed my shoulder. "So you want Mother to know that you drew your hand with the most love?"

I nodded.

Melinda hugged me. "I think Mother will love it. Let me help you wrap it up."

✦ ✦ ✦

"Happy birthday, Mother!"

Supper was delicious. Luisa fixed all of Mother's favorite foods. Since they were my favorite foods too, I ate until I was stuffed. After dinner, we all settled into the parlor to watch Mother open her gifts.

Justin presented her with the beautiful pearl necklace and even some matching earrings.

"Oh, you shouldn't have!" Mother pulled Justin down and brushed his cheek with a kiss. "But I'm glad you did."

"Open mine next!" Melinda begged.

Soon the pink shawl with a pretty design of red roses lay across Mother's shoulders. "It's lovely, dear. Thank you."

Melinda beamed.

"Our turn, Chad," Mitch said. They left the parlor and returned a minute later, struggling with a large, blanket-draped gift in their arms.

Yanking off the blanket, Chad shouted, "Happy birthday, Mother!"

"Chad! Mitch! How perfect." She stood up and ran her fingers lightly over the smooth leather of the new saddle. "How did you know Misty and I were pining for a new saddle?"

"Well, now," Chad teased, "it sure was hard to guess, wasn't it, Mitch? Especially since she kept saying after every ride, 'I wish I had a new saddle.'"

Mother batted his arm in protest. "Oh, you! I did not. Although I might have mentioned it once or twice."

Everybody laughed. I smiled, but I didn't feel like laughing. The other birthday presents were so nice. Mine was so . . . ordinary.

What if Mother doesn't like my drawing, even in the pretty frame?

"I think I have one more gift," Mother said brightly. She reached for the small, square package wrapped in tissue paper and tied with a pink bow. Melinda had made it look pretty on the outside, but would Mother like the gift inside?

Before Mother's fingers could close on the gift, I jumped up and snatched it away. I stood in front of Mother, holding the package against my chest.

"I changed my mind," I said, bursting into tears. "I don't want you to open it. It's not a good present."

"Darling!" Mother patted the settee and motioned me to sit beside her.

I sat down but couldn't stop crying.

"Instead of tears on my birthday, I'd rather see a smile," Mother said. "Do you think you can give me one?"

All my worries poured out at once. "Oh, Mother, I'm sorry! I spent all my pennies on *me*, so I only had twelve cents left to buy you a present. It's not nice at all. Not like a shawl or a necklace or a saddle. You won't even like it."

"I'm sure I'll love whatever you give me, sweetheart."

"But I only bought part of your present at the store. Mostly I made it myself."

I tried to hang on to the package, but Mother gently pried my fingers away. "May I open it and see? Please?"

I sniffed, then gave Mother an unhappy nod.

Mother tore open the tissue paper. "Oh, *Andrea.*"

I saw her eyes. They were filled with tears. One tear dripped down her cheek. "Your father used to tell you that about your left hand."

"You don't like it," I whispered. "I made you cry."

"I'm crying because it's the nicest gift anyone has given me in a long time. It's easy to buy something at the store, but you gave me something from your heart. I'll treasure it always."

"Truly?"

"Truly," Mother promised, and she never lied.

Right away, I felt a lot better about the gift. I was a teensy bit sorry, though, for Melinda, Mitch, Chad, and Justin. Mother didn't say *their* presents were the nicest.

But it looked like they didn't care. Even Melinda smiled at me.

Just then Luisa brought in a big, white cake with shining candles. Everyone sang to Mother. Luisa cut the cake, and Mother let me have first pick.

Chad tried to tickle me to keep me from taking the biggest piece. "That one's mine," he warned with a grin.

I let him have it. Mother was having a happy birthday, after all. And maybe—if I asked Melinda nicely—she could help me save money for Mother's birthday next year.

3
Aunt Rebecca and the Hat

July 1876
This story takes place two summers after Andi's Indian Summer.

AUNT REBECCA LIKED to visit us on the ranch. I don't know why, because all she ever did during her entire stay was complain about the dust, the heat, and the roughness of the surrounding countryside.

Mother said she came because she was lonely. Aunt Rebecca lived in a big old house in San Francisco by herself, with only a handful of servants.

Justin told me she visited because she enjoyed being around family. "She moved out West years ago to be near Father and his family," he reminded me more than once.

But I think my brother Chad had it right: "Aunt Rebecca visits because she likes being in charge and bossing folks."

Chad would know, since he likes being in charge and bossing folks too.

Here on the Circle C ranch, Aunt Rebecca had her whole family to boss, and to make sure we all followed the "narrow way." *Her* way. Since she was old, nobody wanted to hurt her feelings.

Aunt Rebecca liked surprise visits, but most of the time Mother told us ahead of time when she was coming. That way I would not be caught off guard and do something to disgrace Mother.

This was one of those times.

Melinda and I were waiting for Aunt Rebecca to arrive, trying not to muss our matching white dresses. At least *I* was trying not to muss my dress. Melinda hardly ever looked rumpled, even when she first woke up in the morning.

Auntie usually showed up with an umbrella looped over one arm (even in July) and a carpetbag at her feet. Sometimes she came bearing gifts.

That was scarier than her list of rules.

She often brought an article of clothing with instructions on how and when and where it ought to be worn. Like the red, scratchy Christmas dress she brought me when I was six years old. I still get itchy thinking about that dress. Aunt Rebecca had given us our matching white dresses on her last visit. She'd written ahead to Mother, suggesting that we wear them today.

I tugged at the stiff collar and peeked out the window. Aunt Rebecca's carriage was rattling up the driveway to the front porch. I wanted to run and hide in the barn, but Melinda kept a firm grip on my arm. She was thirteen and sure knew how to keep me in my place.

Aunt Rebecca no sooner stepped into the house than she unpacked the gifts she'd brought. My eyes opened wide. She was holding two enormous sun hats. I'd never seen anything like them.

"The California sun is terrible on a young lady's skin," Aunt Rebecca said, all smiles. "These lovely hats will protect you. I had them made especially for you girls."

Melinda and I looked at each other. We didn't say a word. The hats were so large I was sure I'd fly away like a kite if the wind came up. I looked at Mother. Her lips were pressed tight, like she was trying hard not to laugh.

The next thing I knew, Aunt Rebecca plopped that monster hat on my head. "Adorable!" she exclaimed. "Simply adorable!" Then she set the other hat on my big sister's head.

Melinda did not look adorable. She looked silly.

Aunt Rebecca beckoned to someone outside. At her instructions, a man hauled a bulky camera, flash pan, and tripod into the foyer. *A photographer!*

"Come along, girls," Aunt Rebecca said cheerfully. "I want

your likenesses preserved on photographic plates. You each need to stand still for only a few minutes. Then you may go."

"Mother?" I pushed the brim of the ridiculous hat out of my face and pleaded with my eyes for Mother not to go along with this.

Her eyes twinkled. "It will only take a minute, sweetheart." That meant, *Humor Aunt Rebecca, Andrea.*

I stood right where Auntie put me and held the little bouquet of flowers she stuffed into my hand. I hoped with all my heart that my three big brothers would not walk in just then. They would laugh and laugh. My cheeks grew hot just thinking about it.

The photographer disappeared under his black cloth for what

seemed like an hour. "Hold very, very still," he ordered in a muffled voice.

I held still. I felt stiff as a fence post.

Then . . . *crack!* The flash powder blew up and I jumped. The smell of sulfur made me sneeze. I hurried away, waving at the smoke.

Nasty!

Aunt Rebecca took my bouquet and gave it to Melinda. She stood just as still for her turn. When the *crack* came a second time, she skipped away from the photographer and snatched my hand.

"Let's go outside and see if these hats work. The sun is really hot today."

Not a good idea, I thought. I didn't want any of the ranch hands to see me in this getup.

I had no choice. Melinda tightened her grip on my hand and led me outdoors.

The hats worked. How could they not? No sunshine touched my face. That hat was like a big umbrella on my head.

Then the worst happened. I heard a snicker.

I turned around to see Chad standing there with his arms crossed over his chest, grinning. "Well," he said. "Don't you two ladies look . . ." He snickered again. "Um, well . . ."

"Ridiculous!" I yelled.

"That word did cross my mind," Chad said and laughed louder.

Just then the ranch dogs ran up for a greeting. Duke bounded into me, like he always does, and knocked me flat on my fluffy-white backside. Instead of licking me, he froze. He backed up a step and yipped. Then he growled. Before Chad or Melinda or I could stop him, he bit into my hat and yanked it off my head.

"Duke!" Melinda shouted. "No, Duke!"

I started giggling.

Good old Duke. He knew an enemy when he saw one. He held that big, floppy hat in his mouth and shook it, growling low in his throat. He put his paw on the brim and tore at it. Maybe he thought it was some kind of mean animal attacking me.

I sat in the dirt and laughed and laughed.

Aunt Rebecca did *not* laugh. When she saw what was happening, she gave a shriek. Then she rushed down the porch steps and into the yard. "You *beast!*" she hollered, grabbing the precious hat. "Drop it!"

Duke did not obey. He gripped the hat tighter, clearly determined to win the tug-o'-war with Aunt Rebecca.

Rip! A small piece of the brim tore away into Aunt Rebecca's hand. Duke, with the rest of the hat in his jaw, took off. He disappeared behind the barn.

I hope he buries it, I thought between giggles.

Aunt Rebecca started to scold me, but Chad jumped in. He picked me up off the ground and held me in his arms, away from her quick tongue. "It's not Andi's fault," he said. "The dog was too fast. There was nothing anybody could do. I'm terribly sorry, Aunt Rebecca."

Chad didn't look sorry. He looked ready to laugh.

Aunt Rebecca closed her mouth, but I could tell she was still mad. Without another word, she turned on her heel and marched back to the house. As soon as she was out of sight, I looked at Chad. We both started laughing. Melinda joined in.

Thanks to Duke, I was rid of that hat forever.

4
White Christmas

December 1878
This story is set a year and a half before Andi's adventures in Andrea Carter and the Long Ride Home.

Chapter 1

"Why can't it snow, just once?"

I looked through the wide French doors during breakfast a week before Christmas. The rising California sun—though pale—was shining. The temperature had dropped last night, but the water in the horse trough showed no sign of freezing.

Like always.

Chad laughed. "Snow?" He scratched his chin and turned to our oldest brother. "What do you think, brother Justin? When was the last time it snowed on this ranch?"

Justin took up the joke. "I remember it well, brother Chad. I was fourteen. You were thirteen." He grinned. "We ganged up on Mitch and washed his face in one inch of snow."

Mitch did not join in the laughter. "A couple of bullies," he said sourly. "Kind of a mean trick to play on an eight-year-old boy." Then he perked up. "But I got you two back. I—"

"Never mind," I broke in. I'd heard this snow tale before. It seemed like all the fun went on before I was born. I slouched. "I'd sure like to see some snow."

Mother was smiling her I-know-something-you-don't-know grin.

"What?" I asked. "Did the *Farmer's Almanac* predict snow this year for the valley?"

She shook her head. "I'm afraid not, sweetheart. But your brothers have decided to take the day off and head up to the mountains to cut a Christmas tree. They also promised me a supply of cedar and fir boughs to decorate the rest of the house."

Of course they did. Why didn't I ever know these things? *Oh, that's right. I'm only ten. The baby sister. Nobody ever tells me anything.* "Even Justin?" I asked.

"Yep, even me," my oldest brother said with a wink. "Would you like to go along?"

I dropped my fork onto the pile of scrambled eggs on my plate. "*Me?*" It came out as a squeak. "But—"

I clamped my mouth shut before the rest of the words could find their way out. I didn't want to remind Mother there were still three days left before school let out for the holidays. She was real particular about not ever letting me play hooky.

"I'll write a note for Miss Hall when you return to school tomorrow," Mother said. "After all, it *is* Christmas, and this is only a day trip." She turned to Chad. "You'll be back this evening in time for a hot supper, I trust."

"Yes, *ma'am*," Chad assured her with a cocky grin. "We're not going far. Just high enough to find a bushy Douglas or white fir."

"High enough to find some snow," I put in.

"Of course."

"Shouldn't we wait until next week so Melinda can come along?" I asked generously.

My fifteen-year-old sister would soon be home from Miss Whitaker's Academy for the holidays. She was away all year at something called "finishing school" in San Francisco. She'd been gone since last fall, and I missed her dreadfully.

"I'm sure Melinda would rather walk in the door and see everything decorated and smelling like Christmas," Mitch said. "She's never been one to tramp around in the wilderness."

"I am!" I blurted.

"That's why we invited you to go along this year," Chad reminded me with a smirk.

I was so excited I could hardly finish my breakfast. Most years Chad and Mitch made the Christmas tree trip while I was in school. It was a rough adventure—too exhausting for little girls.

Two years ago, the whole family went, but the trip ended a half hour after we left, before we even reached any snow. Melinda started throwing up, so Mother turned around and took us girls home. I cried. Both Melinda and I were sick for Christmas that year.

But, oh, happy day! I was not a little, *little* girl any longer, and I was not ill. I pushed back my plate, pleaded to be excused, and rushed upstairs to ready myself for the all-day adventure into the high Sierra.

+ + +

By the time I clomped down the stairs I felt like a pack mule. Under my overalls I wore a pair of long johns—red flannel underwear—and a flannel shirt Mitch lent me. I'd rummaged through my wardrobe for my only pair of mittens, a scarf, and a winter coat. I carried the pile of clothes and followed the boys out to the wagon.

"In you go," I told my outerwear and tossed everything into

the wagon bed. I piled my snowshoes on top. A saw and a double-bit ax lay nearby, along with a wicker basket full of a picnic lunch. A picnic in December!

Tingles of excitement raced up and down my neck. "Do I get to help pick out the tree?" I asked the first brother who wandered by.

"Yep," Chad said, tossing his winter gear in next to mine. He looked east. The sun had climbed a little higher into the cold December sky. "Perfect day. No fog, sunny, and crisp."

He pointed to the faraway peaks. "See the snow line? It's good and low. You'll see snow, little sister. You can count on it." He ruffled my hair and headed for the barn.

Ten minutes later, the two horses were hitched up to the wagon. I found a couple strings of old bells in the tack room and quickly tied them to the harness. Pal shook his mane, and the bells jingled. Perfect!

I climbed into the back of the wagon, eager to leave. Mother came outside just then. Her arms overflowed with blankets. "Your trip might be more comfortable if you don't have to sit on the hard wagon bed." She handed the blankets up.

"Thank you, Mother." I piled the blankets in a corner and snuggled down. It felt warm and cozy—almost *too* warm. Down here in the valley, the sun warmed me so much I wanted to get rid of my flannel underwear. But I didn't. The boys were in shirtsleeves.

"Have a lovely time," Mother said.

I leaned over the wagon side and gave her a hug. "We will," I told her. "Don't you want to come along?"

"I've had my share of snowy days in the mountains," she said with a laugh. "I'll enjoy the tree and fir boughs when you return. I need to scoot up to the attic and go through the ornaments while you're away. Hurry home," she finished. "Hot chili and Luisa's famous cornbread for supper."

My stomach growled at the thought, even though breakfast had just ended. Chad gave the horses a slap with the reins, the wagon jerked, and we were on our way.

Chapter 2

"Jingle bells, jingle bells, jingle all the way . . ."

The boys and I sang at the top of our lungs in the crisp morning air. The words, mixed with the horses' jingling bells, echoed back from the rolling hills.

I thought we'd sung every verse there was, when Chad—in a clear, deep voice—started singing:

> A day or two ago,
> I thought I'd take a ride,
> And soon Miss Fanny Bright
> Was seated at my side.
> The horse was lean and lank;
> Misfortune seemed his lot.
> He got into a drifted bank,
> And then we got upsot.

The rest of us joined in the chorus. Chad went on and sang the rest of the ballad about a poor fellow who was left adrift in the snow when his sleigh overturned. When he finished, I was laughing so hard that tears trickled down my cheeks. I fell onto the pile of blankets in the back to rest and stared up at the blue, blue sky.

The morning flew by faster than a galloping horse. Pal and Caesar touched noses and gave us a swift trot, at least until the road became too steep to push the horses too hard. I was having so much fun talking and laughing with the boys that I didn't notice the ground had turned white some miles back.

I looked behind me. The wagon had left two long, wide

lines in the snow. At first I could see the brown, winter-dead grass beneath the white. Ten minutes later, the snow was a few inches deep.

Another hour, and the world turned into a sparkling white that hurt my eyes. We had left the valley oak and scrub pine far below. Towering overhead, tall ponderosa pine and fir pierced the sky.

The only time I'd seen such a sight was on a calendar at Murray's hardware store. I liked to flip through the pages and see paintings of faraway places. Now I was seeing those icy places for real. Best of all, they were only a morning's ride away.

For sure, I want to do this every year, I thought. I blew out tiny puffs of air and watched my breath float away. I pretended I was a snow princess traveling to her ice castle up on a high mountain.

I might have sat there for another hour and frozen to death if the wagon hadn't come to a sudden halt. Justin's voice yanked me from my daydreaming.

"Huh?" I asked.

"I said you better get some more clothes on," he repeated. He, Chad, and Mitch had jumped down from the wagon seat and were putting on their coats and heavy gloves.

"I hope you're wearing plenty of extra socks inside those boots," Chad said. "From here on in, we walk."

By now it was nearly noon, and I was hungry. "Can we eat first?" I asked, looking with longing at Mother's picnic basket.

"Might as well," Mitch said with a shrug. "We've got a long hike ahead of us."

We dug into Mother's good roast-beef sandwiches and left-over chocolate cake from last night. The water in our canteens had stayed plenty cold, and soon I felt refreshed and ready to go after that perfect tree.

The reason for leaving the wagon and horses behind soon

became clear. The snow was too deep to drive the wagon, and the road had changed to a narrow path through the forest. At least, I *thought* it was a path. The snow came up past my knees. I had no idea how my brothers knew where to go.

I was panting and trying hard to keep up when Justin held up his hand. "It's time for snowshoes," he said. "We can't keep breaking this path. I'm beat."

Chad snorted. "If you spent more time out on the range working and less time sitting in a lawyer's fancy office, you'd have no trouble breaking this easy path."

It was true. Chad and Mitch looked none the worse for wear. But Justin looked as tired as I felt. The boys took a few minutes to latch their snowshoes to their boots. Justin helped me with mine. I was mighty glad I could wear them rather than carry them.

My joy lasted two steps. One . . . two . . . *plunk!* I tripped over the awkward footwear and fell backward into the snow. "These things are harder to use than I thought they'd be," I complained.

"You'll get used to them quick enough," Chad said. "Come on. Let's move."

We hiked deeper into the forest. Chad was right. I did get used to the funny-looking snowshoes. They were long and clumsy, but with extra determination, I made them work.

Chad and Mitch kept fifty yards ahead of Justin and me. *What's the big hurry?* I wanted to shout. But it was hard enough work to breathe, much less talk. I kept quiet and stayed close to Justin.

I began to suspect that my oldest brother had come along on this adventure to keep an eye on me. Chad and Mitch knew what they were doing and were on a mission. They probably would have forgotten I was along.

"You doing all right?" Justin asked a few minutes later. He pulled me to my feet after another tumble—this time face-first—and helped me brush off the snow.

I nodded. "They'll pick out . . . the tree . . . before I can get there," I said, panting for breath.

Chad's loud voice chased away any worries about that. "Over here!" he yelled. His voice echoed *"over here . . . over here . . ."* and Justin and I hurried to catch up.

When we arrived, Chad was grinning. "Here's our favorite spot for young trees."

He swept his hand across what looked like part of an alpine meadow. Elk and deer tracks were everywhere. Tall trees rose high; younger trees half their height dotted the area, blanketed under a layer of fresh snow.

"Go ahead and pick out a tree, Andi," Mitch urged.

Feeling tired no longer, I spent the next half hour looking over the stand of fir trees. One was too bushy; another too short; some showed elk and deer damage.

Finally, I found the perfect tree. The white fir was probably ten feet tall. It towered over the boys. But it would fit just right in Mother's fancy parlor, where the ceiling rose at least that high.

Chad, Mitch, and Justin agreed it was perfect. They spent the next fifteen minutes scraping snow from around the base of the tree so they could chop it down. Finally, a *zing* then a *whack* told me the tree was coming down. It hit the ground with a muffled *thunk*. Snow flew up and smacked me on the cheeks.

I gasped. "It stings!"

That gave me an idea. The boys were busy trimming the branches and getting the tree ready for towing back to the wagon. While they wrapped the tree up with a long rope, I reached down and scooped up a handful of snow.

To my surprise, the fluffy snowflakes could be packed tightly together. I added more snow until I had a perfect ball. Then I crept closer and closer to Chad. He was down on his knees, tying the final knots in the rope. He didn't see me sneak up behind him.

Quick as lightning, I yanked his coat collar back and dropped the snowball down his neck.

I never saw anybody leap up so fast. He let out a yell that echoed throughout the meadow. Then he shook the snow out of his coat and whirled on me. "I'm gonna get you for that." He gave me a wicked smile.

I ran. Or tried to.

We had taken off our snowshoes to manage the tree, so I ran across the meadow on foot. The snow was deep—too deep to get away. Each step made me sink deeper. My heart pounded.

A triumphant laugh told me Chad had caught up. He scooped me up in his arms and headed back toward Justin and Mitch. They were watching with wide grins.

"Let me down!" I yelled, half laughing, half crying. "I won't do it again. I won't!"

"I bet you won't," Chad said. "Not after today."

I saw his destination—a deep snowdrift just past where we'd

cut down the tree. With a mighty heave, he threw me. I sailed through the air, my arms and legs thrashing wildly. Then *ker-plunk!* The snowdrift rushed up and hit me full in the face. I tried to scream, but snow filled my mouth and nose.

Strong arms almost immediately came to my rescue. Chad plucked me from the drift and set me upright. "Learned your lesson, little sister?"

"Y-yes, Chad," I stammered. "But p-please! Do it again! That was fun!"

Chad shook his head and chuckled. He tossed me twice more then said it was time to get back to work. We strapped on our snowshoes and began the long hike back to the wagon.

I stayed close by, humming "Jingle Bells," while the boys took turns hauling the monster tree down the trail. They also cut spruce and cedar boughs along the way.

For some reason it didn't feel like early afternoon. The sun should have been bright, though it was not very high in the sky. The trees blocked some of the light, but even then, it seemed darker. My shadow no longer showed on the open trail.

I looked up. The whole sky had turned overcast and gray. "I think it's going to snow," I said. This was something I wanted to see. Snow falling from the sky!

My brothers stopped. They glanced up at the cloudy sky, then they looked at each other in sudden alarm.

"A storm's headed this way," Chad said.

Just then, an icy wind whipped down the path, bringing with it a flurry of snow. It felt like a cold knife had just stabbed me through my heavy coat.

I gasped.

Chapter 3

"We gotta go!" Mitch yelped. "C'mon! Hurry!" My brothers dropped the tree and the boughs.

"Go where?" I asked. The wind snatched my words away so nobody could hear me.

Before I knew what was happening, Justin had grabbed me and was ripping the snowshoes from my feet. He picked me up and took off down the trail.

The wind blew at us from behind, coming down off the mountain like a roaring beast. Snow fell everywhere. The wind whipped it up from the drifts and slammed it into our faces; it came from the sky and beat us on our backs.

"What about our Christmas tree?" I shouted in Justin's ear.

He shook his head and plodded on. The wind carried us down the path at a fast run. It was still light enough to see the fir trees. Far ahead, I saw dark, fuzzy shapes. Chad and Mitch were running fast, even in their snowshoes.

Nobody spoke. Nobody told me where we were going or what we would do when we got there. Would we run all the way home? By now I was shivering, and my teeth chattered. "I'm cold," I yelled.

"I know," Justin yelled back. He was panting.

Just ahead I saw the dark outline of the wagon and the two horses. Mitch and Chad were already there. They grabbed the bridles and urged the horses off the trail and deeper into the woods.

Justin, carrying me, followed the wagon. Once in the woods the wind dropped a bit, but I was still icy cold. I clenched my jaw to keep my teeth from rattling my whole head.

I want to go home! I didn't say it out loud. I didn't want to be a crybaby.

I blinked back tears and tried to see through the white wall of snow. The boys had drawn the wagon into a thicket of close-growing young trees. The horses whinnied. It sounded like they didn't like the scratchy branches.

Chad calmed them and set the wagon brake. Then he made

his way to Justin and me. "It's the best shelter I can find for now," he hollered over the wind.

Justin nodded. He put his face close to mine. "Listen to me, Andi. I have to help make some kind of shelter. I'm going to put you in the back of the wagon. Cover up with the blankets and stay put. Do you hear me?"

He dumped me in the wagon bed while he talked. I nodded, suddenly scared—and colder than ever. I burrowed under the blankets, but they didn't help me feel any warmer. A dull, cold ache entered my belly. My head hurt from clenching my jaw against the cold, and I couldn't stop shivering.

It was dark under the blankets. All I could hear was the wind howling and the snowflakes hitting the wagon. Where was Justin? Where were Chad and Mitch?

A sudden bump from the underside of the wagon made me jump. What were they doing?

Time crawled.

Suddenly, somebody yanked the blankets from me. I yelped as icy snow pellets stung my face.

"Come on!" Chad looked half frozen.

I stood up and let him haul me out of the wagon. Where was Chad taking me? The answer hit me a second later. He dropped to his knees and shoved me under the wagon.

Instantly, the wind vanished. It was still cold, but better than before. I was small enough to sit up under the large wagon bed, and I took in my surroundings.

Except for the hole Chad had pushed me through, a wall of snow filled all four sides from ground to wagon bed. The boys had been busy hauling snow to pack around the wagon. Underneath, fir branches were spread on the snow. Mitch took one of the blankets and laid it over the evergreens. I scooted out of the way and let him work.

My brothers worked fast, but the light was nearly gone by

the time they crawled under the wagon for good. They were breathing hard and shivering.

Justin plugged the entry hole and lay back against the wagon wheel. "Now, we wait," he said.

I couldn't see much. The snowy walls kept out most of the afternoon light. Outside, the snow was no doubt piling up. Poor horses!

"Will P-pal and Caesar b-be all right?" I asked.

"They're sheltered by the wagon and the trees," Chad said. "It won't be long before we feel warmer too."

"C-can you build a fire?" I pleaded through chattering teeth. "I'm awful c-cold."

Chad chuckled. "No, little sister. Not unless you want to burn the roof over our heads."

I felt my cheeks flush. *Dumb.*

"Come over here," Justin said. "I'll wrap you up in another blanket."

I groped my way across the ground and soon found myself wrapped up like a mummy. Justin's gloved hands were shaking with cold, but he kept his voice light. "You'll be warm in a jiffy."

I doubted that. I didn't think I'd ever be warm again.

"I don't suppose anybody remembered to grab the picnic basket," Mitch said.

I heard groans from Justin and Chad.

"Anybody feel like going after it?"

No one volunteered.

For a long time, nobody spoke. Slowly, my shivering grew less. So did Justin's. He slouched against the wagon wheel and snuggled me close.

The dark closed in. "Is it suppertime yet?" I asked.

"Probably," Mitch answered from a dark corner. I couldn't see him anymore. The wind moaned. "I think we're in for a long night," he said.

"With the four of us in this snug little igloo, we'll be fine," Justin said. "Bless Mother for throwing in the blankets this morning. We'll stay close and keep warm. Before you know it, the storm will be over."

Justin's cheerful words were met with silence. I didn't like the silence. It was too dark and too quiet, except for that awful, blowing wind. "Tell me a story," I begged.

One by one, Justin, Chad, and Mitch told me story after story of when they were small. My eyelids drooped. Wrapped in Justin's arms, I began to feel warm. I drifted off to sleep.

Chapter 4

The sound of murmuring and scraping woke me up. I felt stiff and cold, but at least I wasn't shivering any longer. I opened my eyes and saw a little light trickling through the snow walls. It was bright enough that I could make out Chad and Mitch. They were digging in the snow.

"Why are you doing that?" I croaked. My mouth felt full of cotton.

Neither brother answered. They were too busy.

"It's been quiet the past hour," Justin told me. "It's morning, and we think the storm has passed."

"What time is it?" When Justin didn't answer, I frowned. "Don't you have your pocket watch?"

He chuckled. "I don't carry Father's pocket watch with me on tree-cutting expeditions. I wouldn't want it to get broken."

Nobody knew the time. Nobody seemed to care. My stomach was excellent at telling time. Right now it told me I was hungry. And thirsty. I felt wiggly too. I wasn't quite sure how to tell Justin I needed to find a tree or a bush . . . and fast.

Finally, I whispered in his ear.

"It won't be long now," he said. "Look."

Chad and Mitch had managed to break through the snow

wall and tunnel even farther. I laughed. All I could see was their feet as they wriggled and crawled through the snow to the outside world. First Mitch, then Chad disappeared.

A minute later, Mitch poked his head back in. "It's beautiful out here. Come and see."

Justin let me go first. I crawled out from under the wagon and through a tunnel in the enormous snowdrift that had blown against the wagon during the night.

Just when I saw a bright, white light, a pair of hands grabbed my arms and yanked me the rest of the way, out into the crisp, sunny morning. A thousand sparkly diamonds danced on the snow and hurt my eyes.

Right behind me, Justin squirmed from the snow tunnel and stood up. He stretched, stomped, and looked around. "Over there." He pointed to a clump of bushes where the snow was not so deep. "Hurry up."

I hurried.

When I got back, Chad, Mitch, and Justin were scraping snow off Pal's and Caesar's backs. The horses whinnied their unhappiness, but they'd made it safely through the night. The trees had given them some cover, and the wagon had served as a windbreak.

They looked ready to go home. I was ready too.

I glanced at the wagon. Snow had filled the wagon box clear up past the edges. Somewhere under there lay the remains of our picnic lunch. It would take a long time to shovel the snow away.

Then I groaned. The shovel was under all that snow.

My stomach rumbled.

Chad looked over from where he was working with the horses. He caught my gaze. "Make yourself useful. Crawl under the wagon and drag out the blankets."

I squeezed back into our hidey hole, which—now that I had

been outside—felt warm and cozy. It smelled like Christmas in there too. It took me two trips to drag the heavy, woolen blankets out into the light. I shook them free of snow and fir needles and laid them aside.

The boys appeared to be in deep conference. They didn't look happy.

"What's the matter?" I asked.

Mitch smiled. "Nothing. We're just figuring out how we'll get home."

"I think you should be figuring how to get our *tree* home." I shaded my eyes and looked up the trail. We'd abandoned our perfect tree somewhere back there. I couldn't see it. I saw nothing but white and more white.

Justin shook his head. "That tree is snowed in, I'm afraid. It will stay there 'til the spring thaw."

Tears welled up. Our perfect tree was buried! I sniffed and ducked my head. *No fair!*

"You wanted to see snow, Andi," Mitch said. He spread his arms wide. "You've seen enough snow to keep you happy for a few years, I reckon."

That's for sure, I thought. It *was* beautiful. Then I sighed. *So was our tree.*

Justin came over and lifted my chin. He smiled at me. "Don't worry, honey, we'll get a tree. It might not be that white fir, but it'll be pretty. Right now we need to head home. Mother is probably beside herself with worry, wondering what happened to us."

I nodded. Justin was right. I didn't want Mother upset just because I wanted to go back for a tree. But how in the world would my brothers get the wagon out of the snowdrift? Even if they managed it, wheels were no good in deep snow. We needed a sleigh.

Chad rigged the harnesses up on Pal and Caesar to keep

them out of the way. "I'm not leaving good leather harnesses out here for some scavenger to steal next spring," he grumbled.

"How are we going to get home?" I asked.

Chad looked at the horses then grinned at me. "How do you think?"

It came to me in a flash. "We're going to ride Pal and Caesar."

"Yep."

Mitch came around from the other side of the wagon. He was covered with snow from head to toe, but he held up the ax. "Found it," he said. "We'll chop down a tree on the way back, where the snow isn't so deep."

I beamed. It might not be the perfect tree, but at least it would be a Christmas tree.

◆ ◆ ◆

It took most of the morning to make our way off the mountain. Caesar had no trouble dragging the tree Mitch cut down. It was lighter than a sleigh and certainly lighter than a wagon.

The two horses trotted side by side. Justin and I rode Pal; Chad and Mitch rode Caesar. The horses' hooves tromped through the deep snow as easily as if they were trotting along J Street in town.

A trace of snow lingered in the foothills. We left the tree there. Chad and Mitch would take a wagon or buckboard back for it, but first we had to get home.

There wasn't a flake of snow in the valley. I shrugged off the blanket I'd worn the whole way back. It was hard to imagine how much snow we'd left only a few hours ago. I'd seen enough. I was ready for sun and plain, old, dry grass on the ground.

We were still a few miles from the ranch house when Chad

whistled and waved. I looked up. A dozen or more riders were headed our way. It appeared Mother had rounded up a search party, and she was the lead rider.

"Thank God you're safe!" she prayed out loud when we rode up.

I slid off Pal, Mother slid off Misty, and we threw our arms around each other. She looked up at Justin.

"Blizzard," he said.

Mother's face paled, but she nodded. "I saw the clouds over the mountains. The weather came up so fast. We had a terrible rain and windstorm." She squeezed me tight. "I was praying most of the night."

"Oh, Mother!" I said. "We found the most perfect tree, but we had to leave it behind . . . and the boys made a snow igloo out of the wagon and snow . . . and they dug a tunnel to get out this morning . . . and—"

Mother smiled and gently laid her gloved hand over my mouth. "You can tell me all about it when we get home. There's leftover chili and cornbread waiting."

The thought of a hot meal shut me up. I scrambled up on Misty with Mother and we headed home.

◆ ◆ ◆

It wasn't a bad-looking tree, not after we put up the decorations: cookies and strings of popcorn; candles and fancy glass ornaments. The tree was so covered in color we couldn't see the broken-off branches here and there. Being dragged through the snow had not done our Christmas tree any good.

Melinda saw the tree a week later and loved it. She liked the story of how we got it even better. Her eyes sparkled at the retelling. I was pretty sure this would be a "white Christmas" story for years to come.

When we gathered around the piano for our yearly carol singing, Melinda started right in. Most of the time we sang songs like "Hark! The Herald Angels Sing" and "Silent Night." This year, though, she began our caroling with "Dashing through the snow . . ."

We sang *all* the verses, especially the ones about the poor fellow who'd been dumped in a snowdrift.

I knew exactly how he felt.

Part 2

The In-Between Years

5
Prince Loco, Chad's Crazy Horse

June 1880
This story takes place a few weeks after the events in Andrea and the Long
Ride Home.

CHAD'S NEW STALLION was a beauty: coal-black but meaner
than a cornered rattlesnake. Of course, I hadn't believed Chad
when he told me the horse was too wild to go near.

Chad doesn't know what he's talking about, I thought. *That
horse will like me. All horses like me.*

Especially if I'm offering them sugar.

All right . . . so sometimes I'm not as smart as I look.

But the story of the black stallion didn't end with me nearly
getting killed.

After my misadventure while trying to recover Taffy, I came
home to discover that I was not the only person Prince Loco
(that's what I called him because he acted so crazy when somebody tried to work with him) wanted to kill. Jake, one of our
ranch hands, was unlucky enough to find himself on Loco's
bad side too.

Chad was letting me watch him work with the stallion, which—I admit—was a gift. I reckon he saw I'd really learned my lesson after those three long, lonely, and scary weeks away from home. I'd turned over a new leaf the best I could. I hadn't forgotten to do my chores for at least two weeks.

I was watching from a safe distance when I heard Chad tell Jake to bring him a halter and a lunge line. Chad stood in the corral with Loco. The stallion's ears were back, but he usually behaved for my brother. Chad gave his special whistle, which brought the horse about ten feet from him. They were sizing each other up.

I wondered who would end up victorious in today's training session. It would be Loco's first lunging experience. I was betting on my brother. He has a gift with horses—even crazy-mean ones like Prince Loco.

Jake came back, halter and lunge line in hand. He opened the gate and stepped into the corral.

"Shut the gate," Chad ordered. His eyes never left Loco.

An open gate was like sugar to that stallion. He was an escape artist and never wasted a moment.

Jake shut the gate and handed the gear to Chad. He didn't look too keen about sticking around and gave Loco a wide berth. Smart fellow, Jake.

Chad had just started putting the halter on Loco—sweet-talking him the whole time—when Loco's head jerked around.

I sucked in my breath. Loco had Jake in his sights. It was obvious he intended to make the ranch hand his next victim. Before I could blink, the stallion reared up, knocked Chad to the ground, and took off after Jake with a scream.

There's nothing more terrifying than a horse's angry scream. Jake *looked* terrified. I never saw a fellow run so fast. Jake didn't bother to open the gate. He didn't even go over the corral

fence. He dove to the ground and slid *under* the bottom rail in a cloud of dust.

Loco's snapping teeth missed Jake's backside by a whisker. I held my breath, scared half to death. I remembered what a narrow escape felt like.

Then I heard laughter.

I looked over toward the corral. Chad was sitting on the ground, covered with dirt, laughing his head off at the sight of Jake. The ranch hand lay face down in the dirt. He looked thankful to be alive.

Loco reared up and whinnied, no doubt furious at missing his target.

Eventually, everything got back to order. Loco responded to Chad's whistle and settled down. Jake staggered to his feet and passed a shaky hand across his forehead. He glared at his boss and said something too low for me to hear.

With a teasing grin, Chad tossed Jake his hat and went back to working with Loco.

When Jake passed me, I didn't say a word.

✦ ✦ ✦

Three months later, our family headed for the California State Fair with Prince Loco in tow. Nobody trusted that animal except Chad. Mother made me promise to stay away from the horse barns this year. Even Mitch, who is nearly as good with horses as Chad, kept his distance.

"Why you insisted on bringing that black beast to wreak havoc at the fair is a mystery to me," Justin said. "He'll most likely kill somebody if you're not careful. I, for one, do not want to defend you in court against the victim's family if that happens."

Chad laughed. "You leave Loco to me, big brother. He's unpredictable, but I'm telling you this horse can *run*. He's going to help me win that five-thousand-dollar purse this year, or my name's not Chad Aaron Carter."

"I believe you, Chad," I said, grinning. I'd watched him ride Loco this past month. The horse was a streak of black lightning . . . and just as unpredictable.

"The best thing would be to sell that animal before we live to regret it," Mother suggested. "You won't get out of him all the time and effort you've put in, I'm afraid. Perhaps the knacker-man will show up, and we can leave Loco in Sacramento."

"Mother!" Chad looked horror-struck at the idea of selling Loco to the slaughterhouse. "I'm telling you, I have everything under control. You all go along and have a good time wandering around the fairgrounds. I'll tend to Loco."

"You'd better," Justin said. "Don't you dare leave him with any green stable boy."

Chad snorted. "You mind your law practice, and I'll mind our livestock." He turned on his heel and headed for the railroad car, where his stallion had been traveling the past day. For safety's sake, Loco had an entire cattle car to himself.

The fair was, in one word, *hot*. Not much shade, unless you paid a nickel to go inside the tent of one of the dozens of sideshows. It was almost worth the nickel just to get out of the sun.

This year the fair included a strange collection of human curiosities: a tiny man no taller than my knee; a fellow who could swallow a sword; and somebody who could lift more than a dozen men while they stood on a board. My eyes nearly popped out of my head at the sights!

Mother let Melinda and me go around the fair on our own, so long as we promised not to bother Chad. I promised, and we had the week pretty much to ourselves.

Most of the hall exhibits were the same as always—dull. I didn't spend much time looking at displays of cut flowers and vegetable seeds. I didn't waste my money on games of chance either. I did give in and follow Melinda around the sewing and craft buildings. She'd entered a quilt she'd been working on all year and was hoping for another first-place prize.

She'd probably win. Melinda is an expert seamstress.

♦ ♦ ♦

The horse race took place the last day of the fair. It was the most exciting event I'd ever watched. It took a while, but Chad got Prince Loco lined up on the starting line without killing anybody.

Justin looked relieved.

When the starting gun went off, Loco reared then came down at a gallop. It looked like his hooves didn't even touch the ground. It was a one-mile race, and Loco flew out ahead of the pack. Along with a dozen other entries, the governor of California had brought along one of his best horses to compete in this year's race. Governor Perkins's horse was fast!

Near the end of the race, Prince Loco and the governor's horse ran neck-to-neck. I screamed so much that my throat turned raw. I couldn't hear myself, on account of eight thousand other folks in the grandstand were screaming too.

And what do you know? Prince Loco won fair and square. He leaped ahead of the governor's horse at the last second and won by a nose. Chad won the five-thousand-dollar purse. He looked pretty proud of Loco right then.

When the race ended, our whole family ran out onto the track and hugged Chad. Governor Perkins came out of the grandstand and shook Chad's hand. "Nice race," he said graciously. His horse had come in second place.

"No hard feelings?" Chad asked. The governor's fancy thoroughbred had been favored to win today.

The governor laughed. "None at all."

Then Chad surprised me—and shocked Mother. In front of everybody, including the governor, he tossed me up on Prince Loco. It was my first time on his back, and I can't say I wasn't scared. I was. I'd been Loco's victim last spring; I did not want to repeat the experience.

To everyone's astonishment, Loco behaved like a lamb. I reckoned Chad wanted to show any potential buyers that Prince Loco wasn't *loco* anymore—not if a young girl could sit safely on his back.

Mother looked horrified, and not just because I was wearing my Sunday best. But I was just as proud as Chad that the mean old stallion was finally good for something.

Just when I didn't think I could be surprised by anything else, Governor Perkins offered to buy Prince Loco. It wasn't uncommon for folks to buy and sell prize-winning livestock at the fair. The governor clearly wanted to snatch Loco up before somebody else did.

"Believe me, George," Justin warned him. "You don't want this horse."

"Oh, but I do!" Governor Perkins smiled up at me. I smiled

back. Then he made Chad an offer no sane person could refuse. My mouth dropped open at the amount.

"I'll work up a hold-harmless waiver and make him sign it before you turn Loco over to him," Justin told Chad with a wink.

The governor laughed and slapped Justin on the back. "No worries, my friend. I have plans for this horse . . . big plans. I have a number of excellent trainers. This horse has potential, and can he ever run!"

We came home from the fair a lot richer than when we went. I'm not sorry Prince Loco is gone. I know Mother is glad too. He'll probably end up a famous racehorse somewhere back East. The governor of California has a lot of racing contacts back in the States.

I wonder if they'll keep his name. "Prince Loco" doesn't sound like a very dignified name for a champion racehorse.

6

Hurrah for the Fourth of July!

July 4, 1880
This story takes place on the Fourth of July before the events in Andrea
Carter and the Dangerous Decision.

Chapter 1

"Hurrah, hurrah for the Fourth of July!"

I slid down the banister before anybody—namely Mother or Luisa, our housekeeper—could catch me. I was decked out in a white and navy-blue middy blouse and skirt. Melinda had just finished doing up my hair in loopy braids with red ribbons.

It was seven o'clock on a bright, already-hot July morning.

"Happy Fourth of July!" I greeted my family at breakfast.

Justin looked up from his plate of hotcakes and whistled. "You look like a true niece of Uncle Sam today, honey," he said. "All you need is a flag."

"I'll get one in town later." I flopped down in my seat. Melinda entered the dining room right behind me wearing a new, green-and-white summer dress.

"You all slicked up for Jeffrey?" Chad teased.

"Wouldn't you like to know!" she shot back, laughing.

Nobody seemed to care that we girls were late for breakfast.

Everybody looked cheerful and ready for the big celebration. Chad had let the ranch hands off for the day; a few old-timers volunteered to stay behind and keep an eye on things.

"I have a surprise for you, Mitch," I said between gulps of milk.

Mitch raised his eyebrows. "Oh?"

I nodded. "You oughta take a look at Chase. Before the sun came up I went out and braided his mane and tail. Then I tied red, white, and blue bows on—"

"You *what*?" Mitch choked on his coffee.

"I fixed him up to look like the champion he is," I explained. "He's sure to win the Fourth of July race this year. He's not named 'Chasing After the Wind' for nothing, you know."

"Andi!" Mitch's face reddened. "I'm not gonna let my horse look like a pampered fool in front of the entire town of Fresno this afternoon."

"Aw, please, Mitch?" I begged. "You're the only one from the family racing. I want Chase to look beautiful when he crosses the finish line ahead of all those slowpokes." I gave him my sweetest smile. "Please?"

Silence. This was a good sign. It meant Mitch wasn't truly angry with me.

"Sure, little brother," Chad put in. "You can borrow a red shirt from one of the dandies in town and—"

"Excuse me, Mother." Mitch rose from his seat in a hurry. "I need to tend to my horse."

Laughter exploded.

I frowned. It had taken me two hours to comb Chase's mane and tail and tie all those ribbons. I hoped Mitch would let them stay in place.

When I went out to the barn after breakfast, Mitch was still tending Chase. He'd curried him till he shone, and he'd left the ribbons in.

"They don't look too bad," he admitted when I thanked him. "I reckon it's the least I can let you do to be part of the race. I know you're itching to ride."

Mitch spoke the truth. I wanted to race so badly it hurt. Two things prevented me. The most important hurdle was my mother. She would not look favorably on me racing in town against the men and boys.

The second obstacle was more practical. If Mitch participated, then what was the use? Chase was the fastest horse in the valley, faster than Taffy. Even with my lesser weight, I could never beat my brother.

I would be content to let a Carter claim the victory and the ten-dollar purse. Maybe Mitch would split it with me for all the work I'd done to get Chase ready for the race.

Mitch let me help him tack up Chase and lead him out of the barn. Chad had the surrey ready to go, with Pal and Caesar harnessed. The last thing I wanted to do was ride to town in the surrey, but Mother gave me no choice. I flashed an I'm-sorry glance at Taffy, who whinnied from her stall.

We arrived in Fresno by mid-morning. Already the thermometer was touching eighty-five degrees. Mother made me wear a straw hat to keep my head from frying. I stood along J Street with at least five hundred other citizens to wait for the procession.

At half past ten, the parade formed under the guidance of the grand marshal, Mr. T. P. Pickering. He started by on his white stallion.

"You and Mitch should be out there too," I told Chad. I wouldn't have said no to riding Taffy in the procession either. Mr. Pickering looked grand on his steed.

"It's too hot," Chad said and stepped farther back under the awning of Goodwin's Mercantile.

He had a point.

A few ranchers and their families had come up from Visalia to join Fresno's festivities. I spotted Liberty Flanders. "Howdy, Libby!" I shouted.

The Triple L ranch had decorated a buckboard wagon and hitched up two draft horses. Libby, her family, and a few ranch hands sat on bales of hay. They looked hot but happy.

"Maybe next year the Circle C ranch will make a float," I hinted.

Chad laughed and shook his head.

Dozens of wagons made up the procession. The hook-and-ladder fire truck passed us, followed by the new steam fire engine. A team of shiny black horses with bells on their harnesses pulled it. They trotted along, clearly not minding the heat.

A few more decorated buckboards rolled past, and then the National Guard marched by. All those boys in blue looked handsome . . . and sweaty.

The Fresno Brass Band brought up the rear, marching in time and playing "The Star-Spangled Banner." I felt so proud to be an American right then. I waved the flag Jack Goodwin had given me earlier and sang along with the rest of the town.

The band marched all the way to Courthouse Park, where there would be more music later in the day and lots of speeches.

"Look," Justin said. "The firemen are going to give us an exhibition of the new engine."

Just in time. I was roasting.

With the pressure from the steam engine, the firemen shot

cold water from the city's waterline up and over the highest building in town. Water spewed from the nozzle, showering the crowd with welcome raindrops. I took off my hat and let the water stream down my face.

As soon as the water turned off, Mitch left.

"Where are you going?" I asked.

"I need to check on Chase. It's pretty hot. I want to make sure he gets enough to drink well before the race." The race wasn't until late afternoon, right after the baseball match between Fresno and Madera.

I tagged along behind Mitch, just to make sure he didn't have second thoughts about yanking the ribbons from Chase's mane and tail. When I caught up, I could tell something was wrong.

Dreadfully wrong.

Chapter 2

Mitch was bent over, with Chase's right forefoot grasped in his hand. His other hand was working the hoof pick. Where he got it was anybody's guess, but I suspected he carried it around in his back pocket.

I peeked at the hoof. "What's wrong?"

Mitch poked at Chase's foot another minute before answering. Then he released his horse's foreleg and straightened up. "It looks like Chase picked up a rock when I rode him into town this morning."

"You got it out, right?" I looked at Chase and my stomach turned over. The sorrel gelding was favoring that foot. He didn't put his full weight on it.

"Yeah," Mitch said. "But it's been lodged in there all morning. I only noticed it now." He shoved the hoof pick back in his pocket and gave me a sorrowful look. "He's out of the race."

I gasped. "No, Mitch!"

"It's not worth it," my brother said. "Chase needs to take it easy the rest of the day."

This was dreadful! Who would represent the Circle C ranch in the Fourth of July race? A Carter nearly always won. "Can Chad race?"

Mitch shook his head. "He doesn't have Sky in town." He reached out and tugged one of my looped braids. "Don't take it so hard, sis. It's only a race."

Only a race! If a Carter didn't win, then Cory Blake might. Or Tom McMurray. His bay was fast.

I fisted my hands and nodded. "I know," I whispered. Then I smiled. "I better get back."

But I wasn't going back to my family. I was going out to the ranch.

◆　◆　◆

I didn't stop to think. I ran all the way to Blake's livery stable, dodging bystanders on the boardwalk. "Mr. Blake!" I hollered into the darkened livery. What if he and his family had taken the day off like most of the town?

Thankfully, he appeared from inside the dim building. "You run around like that much more, Andi, and you'll get heatstroke," he warned. "What do you need?"

"A horse," I said, panting. "I need to go out to the ranch and fetch Taffy. I'll bring your horse back as soon as I can."

Mr. Blake's eyebrows shot up. "Why? What's the matter?"

"Something awful," I said. "Mitch can't race Chase today, so I—"

Cory's father chuckled. "I understand. Wait here."

When Mr. Blake brought me a pinto, I scrambled up on his back. "Thanks!"

"Don't run him too fast in this heat, you hear me?"

I promised I wouldn't and set off trotting down the street. My white and blue middy blouse flapped in the breeze.

◆ ◆ ◆

An hour later, I led Mr. Blake's pinto into our barn and turned him over to Diego, who had stayed on the ranch to enjoy a quiet, restful day with Luisa. He frowned in suspicion when I came out of the house a few minutes later dressed in my old, familiar overalls.

"*¿Adónde vas?*" he asked. "Where are you going?"

"*Al pueblo,*" I shot back. I needed to get back to town as fast as I could, before he or Luisa dragged me off Taffy and into the house to change into my skirt and blouse. I jammed my carefully braided loops up under my hat and touched my heels to Taffy's sides. She was raring to go, having been cooped up in her stall all morning.

I kept Taffy to an easy lope, not wanting to tire her out before the race. When I got to town, the main streets were nearly empty. Everybody was out at the ball field watching the Fresno Centrals beat the stuffing out of the Madera club. It would be a quick game, and the crowd would return soon.

I gave Taffy her fill at the watering trough and then walked her in the direction of the starting line. I tied her to a hitching rail under a large oak tree some distance from the track and made myself scarce.

If Mother saw me, she'd have a conniption fit. I took a deep breath and convinced myself that getting on Mother's bad side was worth representing the Carter name in this all-important race.

By the time the ball game ended, I was sitting astride Taffy along with a dozen other riders. Many onlookers had dribbled away because of the heat. A few riders had dropped out of the race as well. There was no shade on Fresno's temporary racetrack.

The quarter-mile dash is my favorite. It appeared to be some other riders' favorite as well. Tom McMurray slipped in next to Jeff Hopkins. Neither man paid any attention to me. If they recognized Taffy, they didn't say so.

"What are you doing?"

I jerked my head around. Cory had maneuvered his chestnut, Flash, right beside me.

"Racing. Same as you."

His eyes were huge. "Are you *loco*? You're a . . ." He swallowed.

"A girl?" I said.

He nodded.

"Well, don't spread it around," I said. "I didn't see any rule that said girls can't race."

"But—"

"Chase picked up a rock, so I'm racing Taffy in his place." I narrowed my eyes. "I intend to win."

Cory didn't get a chance to reply. Grand Marshal Pickering held up a pistol and told us how many times we had to circle the track. Then *bang!* The starting gun went off.

I felt a surge of relief. No one (like Justin) had dragged me off Taffy before the race began. It was too late now. I would win this race and make my family so proud that even Mother would be glad I'd entered.

I hoped.

Chapter 3

A quarter-mile race is short and fast. Taffy was bred for it. She's a quarter horse. Long-distance running was not her specialty, but she would give her all for the quarter-mile.

She did.

Not even Flash could keep up. Only Mr. McMurray's horse,

Maggs, came close. By the time we circled the track the required number of times, Taffy and Maggs were racing neck-to-neck.

My weight gave me an edge over Mr. McMurray. He was six feet tall and probably tipped the scales at two hundred pounds. I was just a little thing. To Taffy, I weighed almost nothing.

Taffy and I crossed the finish line and won by a length. My heart nearly burst in pride at my palomino's ability to beat the men and boys in the quarter-mile dash. I glanced around to see if anyone from my family had watched the race. Part of me wanted to see the expressions on their faces when they saw the winning horse streak by. Part of me hoped they'd missed it.

When I trotted up to Mr. Pickering and dismounted, he dropped a shiny gold coin in my hand. "Well, missy, that was quite a surprise. Your mother will no doubt have my hide when she finds out I let you race."

Very likely, I thought.

He frowned. "If I'd seen you before the gun went off, I would have removed you and your horse from the race. You know that, don't you?"

I clutched my ten-dollar gold piece and nodded. "Yes, sir."

Then he broke into jolly laughter. "You beat 'em all, Andrea Carter. Every man jack of 'em." He bent close to my ear. "A grand race. Whoever bet on you won a pretty penny."

I reddened. Double trouble. I forgot that folks bet on which horse would win. To be part of the gambling made my stomach drop to my toes. I wanted to grab Taffy and get out of town, preferably before my family realized I'd not only raced, but had *won* the race.

Too late.

"Andrea Rose Carter," my mother said when she saw Taffy and me standing in the midst of the other riders. Her gaze took in my rumpled overalls and wide-brimmed hat. She was not smiling.

"Hello, Mother," I said softly. My hands were so slick with sweat that I almost lost the prize money. I slipped the coin into my pocket.

Mother's disapproving gaze swept over the group of hot, sweaty riders.

"Ma'am," Tom McMurray greeted her, touching the brim of his hat. The others followed, including Cory and Mr. Pickering.

Mother nodded a polite response then grasped my arm. I reached for Taffy's bridle.

"Leave her," she said. "Chad will take care of your horse. You will come with me."

I glanced at Chad, wide-eyed. He caught my gaze and slowly shook his head. *Yep, you're in a heap of trouble*, his look warned.

"Let me explain," I said, scurrying to keep up with Mother's tight grip. She could walk fast and still glide along like a lady. "Mitch's horse couldn't—"

"No, Daughter," Mother said, letting me go. A hint of frost edged her voice. The hundred-degree temperature suddenly didn't feel very warm. "What you did was unseemly and"—she scanned my outfit once more—"you disobeyed me by wearing that attire to town."

Mother was right. I ducked my head and stumbled behind her. I knew I wasn't to step a foot off the ranch in overalls. "It was an emergency—"

"We will not discuss it further," Mother cut in. "You are in disgrace."

Tears welled up. Like Justin, Mother could shame me with just a few words. "Yes, ma'am," I whispered.

I followed Mother to Courthouse Park, where Melinda and Mitch had spread our quilts and laid out our picnic supper. Mitch flashed me a sympathetic look before rummaging around in the wicker basket for the cold chicken and biscuits.

I apologized about a hundred times to Mother in front of the rest of the family.

Mother finally smiled at me. "I forgive you, Andrea," she said with a sigh. "But when are you going to learn to stop and think before you plunge into another poor choice?"

I winced. I often asked God to help me with that, but I never slowed down long enough to give Him a chance to answer. "I'll try, Mother," I promised.

It was true. I really did want to do right.

"Give Justin the prize money," Mother said a few minutes later.

My jaw dropped. "But I—" I clamped my mouth shut at Mother's look and dug into my overalls pocket for the money. I looked at the shiny gold eagle. Ten whole dollars.

"*Now*, Andrea."

I took a deep, regretful breath and handed the money over to Justin. *A fitting punishment*, I thought sorrowfully.

By evening, things had cooled down, both in town and with Mother. She treated me like the incident was over and done with.

"I love you, sweetheart," Mother whispered just before Grand Marshal Pickering read the Declaration of Independence. "I want you to grow up to be a godly young woman who makes good choices." She smiled. "I know you love to race Taffy, and I'm not opposed to you racing. But please! No more racing on the Fourth of July."

"Yes, ma'am. No more racing on the Fourth." I smiled. "I love you too."

After the Declaration, three more men stood up and made speeches about our grand country. We cheered every few sentences.

Then the band played "America" and another round of "The Star-Spangled Banner." In spite of the heat and getting into trouble earlier, I got goose bumps up and down my arms at the songs. It was *that* moving to be with other like-minded folks who loved America.

I looked at Melinda. She had tears in her eyes.

Afterwards we waited for dark. I was so tired that I dozed off. Mitch shook me awake a couple hours later. "You don't want to miss this," he said with a grin.

Indeed not! I sat up just as the National Guard shot off a cannon. Then we watched a fine display of fireworks, the best ever. My gaze was fixed on the flowery sparks of red, green, and blue.

I almost missed Mitch's soft whisper in my ear. "It was a swell race, little sister. I saw the whole thing. You beat 'em all." In the glow of the fireworks I saw him wink at me.

Hurrah for the Fourth of July!

7
A Matter of Honor

This spin-off story is inspired by the events in Andrea Carter and the
Dangerous Decision, *when Andi dreads having to entertain Virginia for
the afternoon.*

"WILL YOU TALK TO *Mother, Justin? This once? I promise I'll—*"

"*I'm afraid this is one area over which I have no influence.
Even Father bowed to Mother's wishes when it comes to entertaining guests. If you knew how often Chad and I got our backsides
tanned for misbehaving when unwelcome guests came calling . . .*"
A smile pulled at the corners of his mouth.

"*Tell me, Justin!*"

"*The time I remember best was when Chad stuffed Freddy
Stone's foul mouth full of dirt and tossed him into the horse trough.*"
*He chuckled at the memory. "Freddy was one of those annoying
little boys who dressed like a sissy and behaved perfectly around the
adults, but he played dirty tricks on the other kids. Chad decided a
whipping was a fair price to pay for entertaining Freddy in a way
he'd never forget.*"

No matter how many times I pleaded to hear the entire Freddy

Stone episode, Justin remained tight-lipped. It wasn't until a few months later, after our sister Katherine had come home to the ranch, that he finally agreed to tell me the story.

It was worth the wait . . .

September 1862

"Children, your attention please," young Miss Hall said that bright September morning. "We have a new student with us this term. I'd like you all to say hello to Katherine Carter. She is Justin's and Chad's younger sister."

Eighteen students chorused, "Hello, Katherine."

From his seat near the back of the room, Justin watched his little sister fidget. Kate might be a firecracker at home, but right now she looked shy, scared, and small for her seven years. She'd been awful sick with scarlet fever last winter. Mother had kept her home from school an extra year to regain her health.

One row ahead and to Justin's left, Chad leaned in to whisper something that drew a sneer from his unruly seatmate. Freddy Stone was known to torment new students, especially little girls. Kate, with her eyes downcast and her hands clasped tightly in front of her crisp, white pinafore, marked her as a perfect target for Freddy.

Chad had better warn Freddy what's what, Justin mused. *And I'll watch them both.* He would keep an eye on Freddy to make sure he minded his manners around Kate, and he'd keep his younger brother from beating the stuffing out of Freddy if he didn't behave.

It was a mystery to Justin's logical, ten-year-old thinking why Miss Hall would seat the two boys together. The tiny schoolhouse in Millerton wasn't big enough for both a mean-mouthed sissy and a hothead.

The teacher laid a comforting hand on Kate's shoulder.

"Katherine, you may sit next to Molly Stevens right here in the front row. Your mother's note tells me you're already in the First Reader."

"Yes'm," Kate whispered.

Miss Hall, who'd often been accused of having eyes in the back of her head, snapped around from settling Kate beside Molly. "Chad Carter! I want that peashooter and those pebbles on my desk at once."

Sheepishly, Chad got up, scuffed his way to Miss Hall's desk, and laid his treasures down. On his way back to his seat, Justin gave him a dark scowl. *Wait 'til Father finds out about this*, he mouthed. Chad had been warned about taking that peashooter to school.

Chad rolled his eyes at Justin.

"You might take Katherine as a lesson, Chad," Miss Hall said. "Just seven years old and already in the First Reader. If you don't start applying yourself, your little sister will not only catch up but surpass you."

Chad flushed. His lagging behind in all subjects was a sore topic both at home and at school. Flinging himself down in his desk, he glared at Kate.

Justin wrinkled his forehead with suspicion. He knew what his brother was thinking: *Teacher's pet already!* Chad would defend Kate to his dying breath if another boy teased her, but he was not above getting back at her himself, especially if she made him look bad. Chad bent over his slate and started scribbling.

He's up to something, Justin thought. Whether it was revenge on Miss Hall for shaming him about his schoolwork or slipping a frog into the Carter lunch pail just as Kate reached for a sandwich, Chad was planning something he shouldn't.

Justin looked at the clock. Three hours until noon. He sighed. Whatever Chad was up to, he'd have to wait until then to find out.

Some time later, absorbed in reading about ancient Rome, Justin became aware of a whispering buzz. It took him a moment to come back from his book. Eyes narrowed in annoyance, he lifted his head to look around the room. Near the front with the little students, Robbie Porter was snickering and pointing across the aisle at Kate.

Justin frowned. *What's so funny?*

Chad sat straight up in his seat, his face as red as Mother's tomatoes. He looked horror-struck. Beside him, Freddy didn't try to disguise his glee at Kate's shaking shoulders and quiet, whimpering sobs. Hand over his mouth, Freddy snorted so loudly that Miss Hall looked up from listening to the Third Reader class.

Chad jabbed his elbow into Freddy, turning the snort into a painful grunt.

"That's enough." Miss Hall rapped her ruler on the desk for order. Silence descended, except from Chad's desk, where Freddy's grunts had turned to yelps. "You boys stop that rowdy behavior this instant."

Glowering at her pupils, the teacher stood up and walked toward Kate's desk. Molly scooted to the edge of the double seat. Puzzled, Justin studied Kate and wondered what had happened to make Chad turn red and the rest of the kids laugh.

Miss Hall knelt and talked quietly while Kate bowed her head in shame. It didn't take Justin long to notice the puddle under Kate's desk and to realize what had occurred.

"Martha," the teacher spoke to one of the older girls, "would you please get a mop and clean up this spill?" Holding out her hand, she led Kate between the rows of seats and into the cloakroom at the back of the classroom. Silent tears streamed down Kate's face.

As soon as the door clicked shut, Freddy began to howl and

slap his desk. Snickers rippled through the classroom. Justin felt heat creeping up his neck. Why hadn't Kate asked Miss Hall to use the privy? She wasn't a baby. Even four-year-old Mitch at home was past having accidents.

Then Justin paused, ashamed, remembering his own first day of school. He'd eaten everything in his lunch pail on the way to school and lost it all over his desk when the teacher asked him to spell his name. Sudden sympathy for his little sister washed over him. He exchanged an uneasy look with Chad. What should the Carter brothers do about this awkward situation?

When Freddy poked Chad and said, "You better find a diaper for your baby of a sister," Justin knew what *this* Carter brother had to do—stop Chad from smashing Freddy's nose into the desktop. He sprang from his seat and caught his brother just in time.

"Simmer down," Justin hissed. "Punching Freddy's not worth a licking."

Chad ground his teeth. Justin held on. He knew just how Chad felt. But any boy who tried to settle up with the blond, curly-haired sissy soon found himself on the wrong side of the grown-ups.

Freddy could put on the face of a sweet cherub quicker than a bee could sting. What grown-up wouldn't believe a darling little boy whose eyes filled with tears when he proclaimed his innocence?

Freddy slouched in his seat and grinned like a possum at the two brothers. He folded his arms across his spotless white shirt and dared them with a smirk to touch him. Then he said an ugly word about Kate.

Righteous anger exploded inside Justin. He gripped Chad tighter, mostly to keep from flying into Freddy himself.

The cloakroom door opened, and all three boys froze.

"Justin," Miss Hall called without looking around, "would you please come here?"

Justin let go of Chad and warned him to behave himself. He wondered why he was being called. Surely a grown-up woman like Miss Hall or one of the older girls could take care of Kate better than he could in this situation.

Miss Hall didn't let him wonder for long. Closing the door behind him, she said, "Katherine needs a change of clothes. Is your mother attending the Ladies' Aid Society meeting this morning?"

Justin nodded.

"You need to take Katherine to the church. Then come straight back. If for some reason your mother isn't there, you will have to drive her home. You can use my buggy."

"Yes, ma'am. But, Miss Hall . . ." Justin swallowed. "What'll I tell the preacher's wife when she asks me why I'm there?"

"I'll write a note for you to give Mrs. Morris, and she can fetch your mother," Miss Hall assured him with a smile.

Sighing, but only to himself, Justin nodded. "Yes, ma'am."

He wished he was back at his desk reading his book about the ancient Romans. All the Romans had to worry about was getting trampled in a chariot race or surviving the arena. Life was a lot less dangerous back then. Probably not one of them ever had to walk a damp little girl down the main street of town looking for her mother. He blushed.

By the time Miss Hall returned to the cloakroom with the note, Justin had calmed himself. Feeling guilty for his unkind thoughts, he whispered to Kate, "Don't cry. It could have happened to anybody."

Kate refused to meet his gaze. She sat slumped on the bench near the door and didn't answer.

All the way down the steps and along the long, main street of Millerton, Justin felt awkward. Sister or not, he would never hear the end of it from his school chums for playing nursemaid to the hiccupping little girl holding his hand.

He searched his mind for some cheerful words, but all that came out was, "Chad and I will take care of mean-mouthed Freddy Stone, only . . . we can't do it at school." *I sure hope Chad remembers that*, he added silently.

Kate's lip puckered as she looked up at him. "Will you really?" Hope filled her voice. Then she sagged. "Father will tan your hides if you do."

"Probably," Justin agreed. He squeezed her hand and gave her a lopsided grin. "But this is a matter of family honor."

Kate ducked her head. "Do you s'pose Mother will make me go back to school?" Fresh tears trickled down her cheeks. "I can't. Everybody will laugh at me."

Weary of this whole business, yet knowing it was a real possibility, Justin yanked a handkerchief from his pocket and handed it to her. "They better not. If they do"—he made a funny, fierce face at her—"I'll line 'em up next to Freddy and punch 'em all."

Through her tears, Kate gave him a quivering smile.

Justin made some more faces. Then he promised to buy her a peppermint stick. "But only if you're brave enough to return to school after Mother finds you fresh clothes," he said.

"I will," Kate whispered.

A few minutes later, Mrs. Morris answered the back door of the church, where the town's ladies gathered every Monday morning to talk about aiding the needy. *Well*, Justin thought as he handed her the note, *nobody's in greater need this morning than Katherine Carter.*

The preacher's wife scanned the note and clucked her tongue in understanding. "Thank you," she told Justin. "I'll see to it that Katherine finds your mother. You may return to school."

Justin shuffled uneasily from foot to foot. "Yes, ma'am." He shot a look at his sister, suddenly unwilling to leave her alone. "You gonna be all right?"

Kate nodded. Then she grabbed Justin's sleeve and pulled him close. "Don't forget about the peppermint stick."

"I won't. Right after school." He gently tugged one of her dark braids and hurried off.

Justin didn't realize he'd been sweating until he was halfway back to school. He rubbed his damp forehead and let out a breath. *Sure glad that's over and done with*, he told himself. He slipped into the schoolhouse and into his seat. In no time he was once again absorbed in his history lesson.

When Mother brought Kate by an hour later, Miss Hall smiled. So did Justin. Kate was dressed in a new, pink-and-white-striped dress from Robertson's general store. She looked pretty as a new filly. The rest of the class appeared to be deep in study. No one said a word when Kate sat down.

Justin sighed in relief and cracked open his spelling book. The teacher must have warned the class there would be no shenanigans over his little sister's return.

He had memorized half a dozen words when Walter Martin, who sat in front of him, turned around and slipped a folded scrap of paper onto his desk. Justin opened it and stared at the crude drawing of a stick-figure girl with a puddle . . .

Justin's face burned. Freddy had drawn this. He was sure of it. Just below the picture he read Chad's scrawl: *I'll get Freddy for this on Sunday. You with me?*

Taking up his pencil, Justin wrote with large, dark strokes: **YES**. Then he passed the note over Walter's shoulder and back to Chad.

For the family honor. For justice.

For Kate.

◆ ◆ ◆

There was no need to speak their plans out loud. Justin and Chad understood each other perfectly. They sat still as statues during breakfast on Sunday while Mother gave her family the usual talk about Circle C hospitality toward guests.

Scrubbed and dressed in their Sunday best, the brothers made it through church and the ride home without mishap.

"What's come over you boys?" Father asked when the carriage pulled into the yard after church. "I've never seen you so quiet and agreeable." He chuckled. "Especially you, Chad. You let Mrs. Drake hug you today without making your usual fuss."

"Nothing, Father," Chad said. "I've just got lots on my mind."

Justin didn't miss the catch in his brother's voice. *Guilty conscience? Or worrying about the consequences?* Maybe this Carter-style justice against Freddy wasn't such a good idea.

Just before the Stone family arrived, Justin pulled Chad aside. "You know we'll get our backsides warmed if we go through with this."

"Yeah," Chad said. "But it's worth it to teach Freddy some manners." He crossed his arms. "You gonna tell Father?"

Justin remembered his promise to Kate and shook his head. "But make sure you don't start anything. I can't defend you if you *start* the fight."

Chad threw his arms up and whooped. "Don't worry. We can count on Freddy for that."

Freddy obliged them within the first hour of his family's visit. No sooner had dinner been cleared away and the children sent outside to play than Freddy began his taunting. The sissy boy, who was dressed in velvet knickers and a silk shirt today, had been polite only long enough to impress the grown-ups.

He whipped out his leg and tripped little Mitch before they left the back porch. Mitch jumped up and clenched his fists. "You did that on purpose!"

"Nah," Freddy said. "You got in the way of my leg." He brushed the little boy aside and headed across the yard, where a rope swing hung from a giant oak tree. He climbed on the swing and pushed himself off. "I made up a limerick the other day," he said. "Want to hear it?"

"No," Justin, Chad, and Kate said together.

"No," Mitch echoed.

As the swing flew in a wide arc, Freddy chanted, "There once was a girlie named Kate, who was too much of a baby to wait. She piddled one day in a quite shameful way, then came back to our class very late." He laughed. "Don't you think it's funny? Mama says I have a gift for verse."

"You have the gift of a foul mouth," Justin said, scowling darkly. He glanced at Kate, whose blue eyes had turned round and horrified.

"Here's another one," Freddy went on. "One day when I went to the—"

Smack! Chad's fist connected with Freddy's shoulder. The boy flew from the swing and landed on the ground. Before Freddy could blink, Chad slammed him down on his back and sat on him.

"Augh!" Freddy hollered. "Stop! Get off me, you—" His words came out fast and furious. Most were words the Carter children would have their mouths washed out with soap for saying.

Chad didn't have any soap, so he used the next best thing. He scooped up a handful of dirt and plunged it into Freddy's shrieking mouth. "You like to talk mean and dirty? Let's see how much you can say through a mouthful of *real* dirt."

Chad then yanked Freddy to his feet and dragged the choking, blubbering boy to the horse trough several yards away. One big push landed Freddy in the trough, where his cries were instantly cut off. Chad held him down while Justin pumped the handle. Water gushed over Freddy's head. He spit and gagged and threw up the mud in his mouth and throat.

"If you ever, *ever* talk that way about our sister or any other girl again, I'll give you worse," Chad promised. He leaned over the soggy heap of velvet and silk and grabbed a fistful of curly hair. "That goes for in the classroom too. You hear me?"

Freddy nodded. Tears and dirty water mixed and ran down his face. "B-but my m-mama will see to it that you get p-punished," he stammered.

Chad turned his back on Freddy and headed for the house. "I don't care."

Later, when the commotion died down and the Stone family had gone home—with a much quieter Freddy—Father dragged Justin and Chad into the library and stood them in front of his desk.

Justin hoped for a tongue-lashing only, but he doubted they'd get off so lightly. Freddy had looked a sorry mess when Father fished him out of the horse trough and offered apologies to his hysterical mama. Mother was clearly horrified at her sons' lack of hospitality.

"Who did it?" Father drummed his fingers on the desktop and waited.

Justin and Chad exchanged bleak looks. Then Chad shrugged. "I did, sir."

Father sighed. "I'm not surprised." He rounded on Justin. "You're the oldest. You didn't think to stop your hotheaded brother?"

Justin shook his head. "No, Father. But let me explain. You see, it was a matter of honor . . ."

Ten minutes later, Chad and Father were staring at Justin. In words he hardly knew he had in him, Justin defended his brother's actions with his reasons for pouncing on Freddy.

"So you see, Father," he finished, "Chad had no choice. He

shouldn't be punished this time. Neither should I." He gave his father a pleading look. "I can bring Kate in as a witness if you like."

Father's face lightened. Soon he was smiling. Then he laughed. "That won't be necessary, Son. I've never heard a defense quite like that one, but you've convinced me." He clapped a hand on Justin's shoulder and said, "Have you ever thought of becoming a lawyer when you grow up?"

8

Snakes Alive!

September 1880
This story begins immediately after Andrea Carter and the Dangerous
Decision.

BY THE TIME ANDI *entered the classroom, she felt completely at*
ease. She headed for the desk she shared with Rosa and slipped into
her seat. Gently, she brushed her palm across the top of her desk
and smiled. It felt good to be back. It really did. She lifted the lid
and reached for her books. Her hand curled around a long, wrig-
gling shape.

Andi jerked her hand back. "There's something in my desk,"
she told Rosa. Carefully, she peeked under the lid. A pair of small
beady eyes stared back. A tongue lashed out.

"Welcome back, Andi," Cory whispered over her shoulder. "It's
only Clyde."

. . . Of course, Andi should *have been listening to the Scripture*
reading. It was all about the Golden Rule—"Such a fitting
topic for this morning," the teacher commented between verses.
But Andi's mind was not on the inspiring words the teacher was

reading. All she could think was, What am I going to do about Cory's snake?

Chapter 1

Clyde slithered around in my desk for a full hour. I could hear his dry scales rustling over my papers and copybook. Every time I peeked under my desk top, the reptile's eyes stared at me, never blinking. Since snakes don't have eyelids, that didn't bother me. What did bother me was the pleading look I thought I saw in Clyde's eyes and an occasional imaginary hiss: *Let me out!*

"You'll be out of there soon enough," I hissed back.

Clyde lunged, and I jumped back. The lid to my desk slammed down—hard.

Rosa squeaked. She sounded like a little mouse.

Mr. Foster glanced up from his desk, where he was listening to the Fifth Reader class recite. I could feel him boring his dark gaze into me. Heart pounding, I stuck my nose in my geography book and pretended to be reading about the Alps.

Rustle, rustle.

I couldn't help it. I giggled. I tell you, I got no studying done. None at all.

Finally, noon recess rolled around. Mr. Foster dismissed the class. Now I had a whole hour to sneak Clyde out of my desk and to somewhere safe. The sneaking out part was easy. I grabbed my tin lunch pail, piled my sandwich, an apple, and three molasses cookies onto my chair, then carefully lifted my desk lid. "Come here, Clyde," I coaxed.

By this time, Clyde had decided a school desk was a cozy place to take a nap. He was curled up in a corner, happy as a . . . well, happy as a garden snake can be in such a predicament.

It was easy as pie to snatch him up and drop him into my lunch pail.

Clyde woke up, slithering all over the bottom of the bucket. I slammed the lid on quick before the teacher figured out what was going on and asked questions like, "Why aren't you outside?"

As soon as I clomped down the schoolhouse steps, Cory pounced on me like a coyote on a mouse. "Got him?" he asked.

I hugged the pail to my chest. "Of course I do."

Cory let out a sigh of relief. "That's good. I didn't want Clyde to fall into enemy hands."

He meant Mr. Foster.

"I'll take him now." Cory held out his hand.

"What do you mean?" I asked. "He's mine. You gave him to me, remember? You put him in my desk. A welcome-back-to-school present."

Cory's smile disappeared. "C'mon, Andi. Give him to me. I can run home and be back long before the noon hour is over."

I shook my head. Cory was not getting this snake back, at least not for a while. He had to learn a lesson about scaring folks with his crawly creatures.

"Andi!" He reached for the lunch pail. "I've kept Clyde for two years. He's the best snake I ever had."

"Now he's the best snake *I'll* ever have." I grinned. The look on Cory's face was just right—regret that he'd played such a mean trick on me, especially since I'd been shot and lost my memory. He deserved to sweat a little. I started walking across the schoolyard.

"Hey!" Cory shouted. "Where are you taking Clyde? You're not letting him go, are you?"

"Nope," I replied.

A small group of kids had been attracted to the commotion between Cory and me. Most of the girls were keeping their distance, but the boys gathered around. I showed Clyde to all of them.

They started bidding on him.

"I'll give you three aggies," Davy Cooper said.

"Four!" Jack Goodwin piped up.

Cory groaned.

Pretty soon I would have a bidding war on my hands. It would be fun, but I had no intention of selling my new pet to the highest bidder. "Clyde's not for sale," I told the boys. "I'm taking him someplace safe until after school."

"Where?" Cory hollered.

I just smiled.

Chapter 2

I left the schoolyard in a hurry. Cory was bigger than I was, and if he got a notion to rip the lunch pail out of my hands and steal his snake back, there wasn't much I could do about it.

Cory didn't know that I had already decided to give his snake back. However, borrowing Clyde was too good of an opportunity to let pass. I started to laugh, just thinking about the reaction I'd get when I sprang Clyde on a certain moon-struck fellow I knew.

But that would come later. For now, there was only one safe place in the entire town of Fresno for Clyde—with my big brother Justin. Cory was right about one thing. The snake could not stay in a tin pail outside. The late fall sun was heating the upstairs like a furnace.

If I thought my desk was the best spot for a snake, I would never have taken the risk of sneaking him out in the first place. But one never knew when Mr. Foster might get suspicious and do a desk check. If he discovered Clyde, he'd make me toss him out the window. And it's a long, long way down for a little garden snake.

I knew I couldn't just barge into Justin's office, hand him my lunch pail, and ask him to babysit Clyde until we went home. A tin pail with a snake inside—sitting on the desk—would not make a good conversation piece for a fancy lawyer talking to a client. I also knew what Justin's answer would be if I asked him to stash Clyde in a corner: "No. Get rid of it. I'm busy."

If I could just get past Justin's clerk, Tim O'Neil, I could slip into Justin's inner office, open the filing cabinet, and let Clyde finish his nap in the dark until it was time to go home. He'd be safe and cool in the corner until this afternoon. If I was *really* lucky, Justin would be out to lunch with some fancy client and never know I'd stopped by.

Luck was with me. I looked at the tower clock just as I reached Justin's office on Tulare Street. Thirty minutes left. Perfect. In and out. It was only four blocks back to school. I could settle Clyde and run back to class with plenty of time to spare.

I ran the last few steps along the boardwalk and burst through the door. Tim, as usual, scowled at me and turned back to some boring paperwork. "Your brother is out to lunch," he muttered. "Should you even be here?"

Justin's fussy clerk should have had more sympathy. After all, only a week ago, I couldn't even remember who he was. Losing my memory had been really scary. But right now, there were certain people I wished I could forget . . . like Tim.

I shrugged and clutched my lunch pail a little tighter. "It's all right, Tim. I just need something in Justin's office. Then I'll leave."

Tim rose at my words, but that didn't surprise me. What could a twelve-year-old, troublesome little sister possibly need in an important lawyer's office?

Good question. He asked it.

I ignored his question and walked across the room. Instead of yelling at me like he usually did, I think he suddenly remembered I'd been so sick with amnesia not long ago. Maybe he thought I was having a relapse. Whatever the reason, he returned to his seat.

"Make it quick," he snapped.

I hurried Clyde into Justin's office, closing the door behind me. Then I saw the tall, heavy, wooden filing cabinet. It was just the place to keep a little snake confined until it was time to go home.

Once home, it would be easy to keep Clyde hidden away in my room. Then tomorrow, when shifty-eyed Jeffrey Sullivan called on my sister Melinda . . .

I smiled to myself. *It will be perfect.*

The bottom drawer of the filing cabinet was heavy, and harder to pull open than I thought it would be. I hoped it wasn't filled with reams of paper. There just had to be a small, secluded spot for Clyde.

I put my lunch pail down, kneeled on the floor, and gripped the handle with both hands. Taking a deep breath, I yanked. The drawer moved a few inches. I yanked again.

"What on *earth* are you doing?" An exasperated voice disrupted all of my carefully laid plans. Justin stood in the doorway, glaring at me with his hands on his hips. He looked pretty annoyed.

I jerked back in surprise and fell backward, but not before I knocked the lunch pail on its side. The lid flew off and Clyde made his escape.

A high-pitched shriek told me that Justin was not alone.

Chapter 3

I didn't dare look up to see who was screaming. By her shriek, I knew it was a lady client.

Not good.

I couldn't worry about that right now, though. Not when Clyde had streaked across the floor and gone into hiding under Justin's large oak desk. I scuttled under the desk and after Clyde for two reasons. First, I had to grab that snake before Justin got hold of it. Second, I needed to stay clear of my brother to give me time to think how I could get myself out of this fix.

Justin is pretty patient with me most days, but escorting a lady client back to his office and discovering a snake on the loose is not good for his reputation as a respected attorney. There are few things more discourteous than a reptile slithering around in a fancy office. Not even finding a mouse would be so bad.

By the look on Justin's face, he agreed. I saw trouble coming at me as fast as a runaway train engine. I snatched at Clyde and missed.

Another shriek and a flurry of rustling skirts told me Clyde had found the lady client. I squeezed my way out from under the desk, looked up, and froze in shock. The young lady had scrambled to Justin, and he was *holding her up in his arms*, clean off the ground.

I forgot about Clyde when I realized that maybe—just maybe—this lady might not be a client but a personal friend. Justin was always mysterious (and tight-lipped) about any lady friends he might be interested in. Could this shivering, frightened young woman be someone my big brother was courting?

Andrea Carter, you have really made a mess of things. Right then, I wished the floor would open up and swallow me . . . and Clyde too.

I stared at Justin; he glared at me. Then he gently lowered the pretty young woman into a chair across from his desk and tried to calm her. "It's all right, Lucy," he said with a slight smile. "It's only a harmless little snake." He turned to me. "Isn't that right, Andi?"

I nodded mutely.

Lucy looked like she didn't believe me. She kept staring at Justin as if he was her hope of salvation from all crawly creatures. Her hands shook.

Justin cleared his throat and told Lucy that I was his sister, and that I didn't mean any harm—which was true. Then he told the young lady my name.

I barely listened. I was watching Clyde. He had made his way under the other chair in Justin's inner office, nearly within my reach.

"Andi, I'd like you to meet Miss Lucinda Hawkins from San Francisco. She's visiting her brother, a lawyer friend of mine who has set up his practice here in Fresno. I've invited Lucy to supper to meet the family."

Uh-oh! If one of the boys brought home a lady friend to meet the family, it might mean he was serious about settling down and getting married. But now? Clyde and I might have ruined all of that for Justin.

"Nice to meet you," I mumbled, but my heart wasn't in the conversation. Cory's snake was right there, not six inches away. Maybe if I picked him up and settled him down a bit, Lucy would see he was not a deadly serpent but a sweet little pet.

"I'm delighted to meet you, Andi," Lucy said. She didn't sound delighted. Her voice shook, and I didn't blame her. A surprise snake would set anybody off.

"Why aren't you in school?" Justin demanded suddenly. He leaned back against his desk and crossed his arms over his chest. "Did Mr. Foster catch you with that snake and expel you?"

I cringed. The schoolmaster had not expelled me—not yet—but the noon hour was nearing an end. I had to get back to school in a hurry. I glanced at Clyde. His tongue flicked in and out, and he'd coiled himself under the chair. Here was my chance.

Quick as a wink, I stooped down and caught Clyde up in my hand. I breathed a sigh of relief. It was too late to ask Justin to keep him for me, but at least no one would step on Clyde now. "Look, Miss Lucy." I held Clyde out so she could see he was perfectly harmless. "There's no reason to scream. He's safe."

Lucy had been looking at Justin, but when she saw me holding Clyde she panicked. She sprang from her chair and flung out her arms, slapping my hand.

Maybe she did it accidentally, but the result was the same. Clyde went flying.

"Andi!" Justin hollered. Hampered by Lucy, who had once again thrown herself into his arms, he nearly fell backward across his desktop. "Get that snake and be quick about it."

No one had to guess where Clyde had gone. From the outer office I heard a grunt then a loud *whack!* "Mr. Carter!" Tim called.

From the sound of his voice, Tim had found Clyde. Or rather, Clyde had found Tim. Either way, this was bad news for Clyde. Tim didn't sound scared or annoyed. He sounded determined. As in . . . determined to rid Justin's office of an unwanted reptile.

Another *whack*.

"Tim, *no!*" I shrieked. Then I whirled and flew out the door.

Chapter 4

Tim paid no attention to my shouting. He held a raised broom above his head. One more crushing blow, and Cory's pet snake would be a goner. Poor Clyde was wedged between a cabinet and a corner, probably in shock.

I watched the broom come down. "No!" I raced to the little snake's rescue.

Just before the blow landed, I grabbed the broom and wrenched it out of Tim's hands. Then I fell to my knees and scooped Clyde up. He lay limply, either scared half to death or—most likely—really and truly dead.

Tears stung my eyes. "You *killed* him!" I whirled on Justin's stuffy, irritating clerk.

Tim folded his arms across his chest. "Good riddance," he muttered, just low enough so his boss—my brother—couldn't hear him.

I heard Tim just fine and burst into tears. I couldn't help it. All I'd wanted to do was find a shady spot for Clyde until school was out so I could take him home. Tomorrow I would have dropped the snake down Jeffrey Sullivan's shirt when he came calling on Melinda. Maybe he'd leave her alone once and for all. I didn't trust that fellow and never would.

Even my brother Mitch agreed Jeffrey was a shifty-eyed character with no-good intentions. Mitch would heartily approve of my plan.

But now? I didn't want to play a mean trick on Jeffrey anymore, even if it was justly deserved. I didn't want to teach Cory any lessons, either, about putting snakes in my desk. I just wanted to turn back the clock and leave Clyde in my desk, or hand him over to Cory at recess like he'd asked.

Now, Clyde was dead. What would I tell Cory?

Tears dripped down my face. It was embarrassing to cry over a snake. Mostly, though, I was sad that because of me, Cory had lost his pet in the very worst way.

A hand fell on my shoulder, making me jump. I looked up, expecting Justin to tell me to dry my tears and get back to school. Instead, it was Lucy.

"I'm sorry," she said softly. "I've never liked reptiles, but I shouldn't have startled so badly when you showed me the creature." She gave me a sincere smile, and I suddenly liked her.

I smiled through my tears. "It's silly to cry over a snake." I rose to my feet, wiped my eyes, and turned to Justin. "I'm sorry, Justin. I was going to stash him in your filing cabinet until after school, to keep him away from Mr. Foster."

Justin sighed and shook his head. He didn't look annoyed any longer, only tired, like I'd worn him out with my antics. Maybe I had. It had been a long three weeks since I'd lost my memory and finally got it back. My oldest brother had carried most of the worry about that.

And here I was on my first day back at school, wearing him out all over again.

Justin disappeared into his office then returned with my lunch pail. He handed it to me without a word, but his eyes told me he was sorry the snake had come to such a sad end.

I settled Clyde gently into his final resting place, put on the lid, and turned to go.

"Wait a second, honey," Justin said. He crossed the room and found a pad of paper on Tim's desk. A minute later he handed me a note. "So Mr. Foster won't mark you tardy."

I didn't need to look at the clock to know the noon recess was over. "Thanks," I said and shuffled toward the door. I remembered my manners just in time. "It was nice meeting you, Miss Hawkins."

She smiled, and her face looked real pretty when she said, "Call me Lucy. Will I see you at supper?"

"Of course! I look forward to it."

With the pail in one hand and my note in the other, I left Justin's office and shuffled down the boardwalk one slow step at a time. I had all afternoon to return to class, but I didn't want to go back at all. I didn't want to face Cory. I stuffed the precious excuse in my dress pocket and sighed.

"I'm sorry, Clyde," I whispered. There was nothing I could do but go back to school and hope Cory would still want to be friends.

I kicked at a loose board. Why did I want to teach Cory any lessons, anyway? Truth be told, I liked seeing his funny little gifts in my desk welcoming me back to school. Worse, the thought of scaring Melinda's beau, Jeffrey, suddenly seemed stupid and childish.

Clyde had paid for my dumb idea with his life.

Twenty minutes later I was climbing the steps to the schoolhouse. I didn't know what to do with the snake, but I thought Cory might want to say a few words over Clyde and give him a proper burial.

I clutched the tin pail's handle and made my way up the stairs and into the classroom. Mr. Foster took Justin's note without comment and went back to listening to geography recitations.

I intended to keep my lunch pail on the floor next to my feet, but I couldn't help peeking inside one last time. I slid into my seat next to Rosa and lifted the lid an inch to bid Clyde a final farewell.

I gasped. Staring back at me were two shiny black eyes. A black and red tongue flicked out. Clyde looked quite put out at being back in the pail. "How did you . . ." I whispered, heart thudding. "You're alive!"

The shock of seeing Cory's snake alive and well made me reach into the pail and lift him out. I cracked open my desktop and slipped Clyde to relative safety, right back where he belonged. When the bell rang at the end of the school day, I returned him to Cory.

Cory asked what I'd been up to during the noon recess, but I wouldn't tell him. I figured it was best not to worry my friend over his pet's near-tragic experience.

9
Virginia's Riding Lesson

October 1880
This story is set one week after the events in Andrea Carter and the
Dangerous Decision.

Chapter 1

My friendship with Virginia Foster, the schoolmaster's daughter, started warming up a little after I saved her life. I convinced the escaped convict, Jed Hatton, to take me hostage instead of Virginia. That was a scary time, and losing my memory for three long weeks afterward did not help.

When I *did* get my memory back, Mr. Foster had to force Virginia to apologize for lying about not being able to ride a horse. She was sorry for a lot of things.

So was I, and we did make up.

Virginia's tears the day I returned to school caught me in a weak moment. I offered to teach her how to ride. Looking back, I should have just forgiven her and kept my mouth shut about the riding lessons.

Nearly every day after my promise, Virginia pestered me. "When will my riding lessons commence, Andrea?"

Commence? Really? I rolled my eyes.

I intended to keep my promise, but the thought of giving up a Saturday morning to lead a scared ninny around on Pal made me regret my earlier, hasty words. "Whenever your family arranges with mine to bring you out to the ranch," I said, hoping to put her off.

I figured the arrangements might take some doing. It's a long way out to our spread, and Mr. Foster probably had other things to attend to on the weekends. My family was also busy on Saturdays.

It was possible that Virginia's lesson might be put off until the rains began later in the fall. Nobody likes to ride in the rain, so it might even be put off until next spring. Who knew if Virginia would remember by then?

The very next Saturday, when I was finishing up my chores in the barn, I heard a jingling harness. I peeked out through the barn's double doors and let out a quiet whoop. A large, double-seated rig from Blake's Livery was pulling up into the yard. Cory sat up front driving. He looked a little put out at his early morning errand.

I thought it might be a business acquaintance of Justin's. Cory would have to stick around to haul him back to town in an hour or two, but we could go riding in the meantime. I grinned.

Then I saw two women in the back seat. I smiled even wider. Better and better. They looked like Miss Lucy Hawkins and her mother. Justin could court his new lady friend, and Cory and I might have the entire day before he had to drive the ladies back to town.

The rig pulled closer. When I saw who Cory was *really* hauling, my belly did a somersault. "Good grief," I mumbled to the stabled horse hanging over his half-door and nibbling at my shoulder. "Is Virginia's riding lesson today?"

Apparently it was. I watched Cory help Mrs. Foster and

Virginia from the carriage. Then he led the gray gelding and
the rig to the hitching rail to tie them up. He looked like I
felt—gloomy.

As soon as mother and daughter disappeared into the house,
I made a beeline for Cory. "Nice ride?" I teased.

He scowled at me. "How would *you* like to be jerked from a
morning of currying horses and thinking about a free Saturday
in town to drag two prissy ladies clear out to your ranch?"

I wouldn't like it at all. "Where's the Fosters' rig?"

Cory let out a deep sigh. "Mr. Foster didn't want to drive
them out, and Mrs. Foster doesn't drive. They hired me." He
reddened. "Actually, they hired Pa and he gave *me* the job." He
kicked a dirt clod. "I have to wait around for whatever they've
got to do here."

He eyed me, squinting against the bright morning sun. "Are
you free? Want to go riding?"

"More than anything!" Then I shrugged. "But I have a terrible feeling Virginia is here for a riding lesson. You know, the
one I promised her last week when I returned to school."

"Worse and worse," Cory said.

"For me, I reckon, but not for you." I tossed a braid behind
my shoulder and thumbed toward the cookhouse. "Cook's
breaking in a new assistant. I hear Marty fixes a mean breakfast of flapjacks and coffee. You're welcome to give 'em a try.
He's just finishing up."

Cory's eyes lit up.

"Or," I added quickly, "you could come along and help with
Virginia's riding less—"

"Nope." Cory backed up and raised his hands to ward off
my words. "This was your silly promise, Andi, not mine."

Fine friend you are, I fussed silently.

Then I relented. Cory was right. It was no fault of his that

I'd offered to teach Virginia how to ride. No need to get sore at him. Cory had already spent an hour in the Fosters' company. And chances were pretty good that he would receive no tip when he took them back to town.

"You're right," I said. "Enjoy your breakfast."

I turned and headed to the barn. Maybe I could give Virginia her first lesson and still have the afternoon free. Better yet, perhaps Virginia would be a fast learner and I'd have most of the day to myself.

"Andi!" My friend Rosa's high, clear voice cut through my mental wishing. I whirled. Cory kept walking toward the cookhouse. It was obvious he didn't want to stick around to hear what Rosa had to say about the visitors.

Rosa skidded to a stop, breathing hard. *"Tu mamá—"*

"Yo sé—I know," I interrupted with a sigh. "Mother wants me to come in and meet our guests."

Rosa giggled, her dark eyes full of teasing. *"O, sí, Andi. Creo que Virginia—"*

"Yes, I'm sure Virginia's here for her riding lesson." I was *not* giggling. It was no laughing matter. "Would you like to come along?"

"Yo no." Rosa shook her head. *"Tengo mucho trabajo."*

"I wish *I* had plenty of work to do. I'd rather muck out every stall in the barn than put up with Virginia's hysterical howling if Pal so much as takes one wrong step." I sighed again. "I'd best get it over with. *Gracias.*"

Rosa nodded and skipped ahead of me into the house. She'd already disappeared up the back stairs to the second floor by the time I slipped inside the kitchen entrance.

Mother, Mrs. Foster, and Virginia were waiting in the parlor. I didn't step over the threshold. I tried to stay out of Mother's fancy parlor when I was in my work clothes.

I expected to find Virginia in a riding outfit suited for a beginner—a simple split skirt, something that would not show the dust in case she took a tumble.

That was not what she was wearing.

Chapter 2

My eyes opened wide. Seeing Virginia's getup, I once more wished I'd accepted her heartfelt apology last week and let it go. But no, I had to open my mouth and offer to teach her to ride.

What was I thinking? Yes, I wanted to be friends. Really, I did. I like to get along with folks, even with those who don't always see eye to eye with me. But *this*?

Schoolmasters in our small town of Fresno don't earn a great deal of money for their hard work. Virginia's mother would sometimes help out as a seamstress when Miss Watkins had too many orders to sew. Mrs. Foster was handy with a needle and thread, and her daughters were usually dressed simply but fashionably in calicos. Virginia might want to dress in rich silks and fancy frills, but it would probably never happen on a teacher's salary.

Until today.

Virginia is not much older than I, but she looked years older dressed in her riding habit. I blinked and said nothing. I was thinking plenty though. *That outfit will get her hurt or killed.*

Folds of heavy, navy cloth reached to her ankles. The fabric must have weighed ten pounds. At the very least, it would make it difficult to mount up. A top hat perched lopsided on her head, and two gloved hands poked out from the sleeves of her tight-fitting, tailored jacket.

Worse, she held a small crop in one hand.

That will be the first thing to go, I decided. If she touched

Pal with that little whip, she'd be left in the dust so fast she wouldn't know what hit her.

Virginia looked like she had just stepped out of a fifty-year-old fashion magazine. Where had her mother dug up that horrid outfit? Probably from her grandmother's moldy old trunk in the corner of some attic. I shuddered.

Mrs. Foster must have noticed not only my open-mouthed stare but Mother's too. "It took some doing," she explained, "but I was able to cut down and refit Great-aunt Mercy's riding habit for Virginia." She gave her daughter's arm a proud little pat. "I remember what a dashing figure Mercy cut as a young lady, riding along the cobblestone streets of Philadelphia back when I was a little girl."

As always, Mother was the gracious hostess. She smiled. "I remember similar sights in the city before my father relocated us to San Francisco during the Gold Rush." She paused, as if considering how to break the news to the Foster ladies. "However, Virginia may find that lovely outfit hot and cumbersome, especially under today's sun."

I suppose the habit *was* lovely. It was made of rich, costly velvet, entirely unsuited for learning to ride astride on a hot day. And that was the only way I knew how to ride.

A sudden, horrible thought struck me. Did Mrs. Foster expect me to teach Virginia how to ride sidesaddle? I knew nothing about that, even though it was the only acceptable way a woman should ride a horse. It was the etiquette of the day, but our family often set aside proper decorum in favor of practicality and safety.

Mrs. Foster did not reply to Mother's careful warning. Instead, she slipped an arm around Virginia and gave her a squeeze. "You go along now, darling, and conquer the wild, western steed. Your father assures me you will be safe." She gave me a long, careful look, which I had no trouble interpreting: *My darling baby had better be returned to me safe and sound.*

Virginia untangled herself from her mother's clutches. She looked eager as ever to be free from her overprotective parent. "Can we start right away?" she asked me.

I nodded, and Mother waved us away. "Please sit down," she told Mrs. Foster. "Luisa prepared a delicious coffeecake for your visit. Shall we . . ."

Mother's voice faded away when Virginia clasped my hand and dragged me down the hallway toward the kitchen. She acted like she knew her way around our ranch house better than I did.

Once out of the hearing of our mothers, she sucked in a breath and began fanning herself. "I know it's the proper thing to wear, but honestly! I can scarcely breathe. Great-aunt Mercy's habit could be altered only so much." She took another shallow breath. "Mother had to lace my corset tighter than ever to make the waist fit. I hope I don't have to do much walking."

A corset! Under the yards and yards of fabric, Virginia was wearing a *corset*? The thought of riding a horse in such a tight-fitting undergarment made my head spin in horror.

Was this the reason Virginia was always fainting? She seemed weak and unable to keep up with any games at school, preferring to stand quietly and watch. Now her mother had laced the corset tight enough so she could fit into a musty old riding habit.

This was definitely the last straw.

I shook myself free of Virginia's grasp and ducked into the kitchen, where we could go upstairs without being seen. "Come with me, Virginia. I have to get you out of those clothes or you might not live long enough to enjoy your riding lesson."

Virginia's eyes turned huge. "What do you mean?"

"You can't ride here in that . . . that . . . whatever-it-is outfit from a hundred years ago."

Virginia drew herself up. "Why not? I'll have you know this riding habit was the height of fashion, and it is *not* one hundred years—"

"It will be the cause of your death," I blurted. "I'm not teaching you one thing until you change into something suitable."

"But my mother—"

"Your mother is not on the horse," I interrupted her again. "You are, but you won't be for long if you don't change. Now quit arguing and come upstairs. I have a sensible riding skirt. You can even keep your blouse if you want to. But the corset and the rest of your silly getup have got to go."

Virginia gasped, and her pale cheeks turned pink.

I folded my arms across my chest and stuck to my guns. I would not be blamed for Virginia's injuries or fainting *this* time. A comforting thought slipped into my mind. If she didn't agree to change into something sensible, I would be off the hook as far as teaching her to ride.

We stood facing each other in the middle of the kitchen. Luisa and Nila bustled around us, fixing the morning coffee Mother had invited Mrs. Foster to enjoy. The two Mexican women chatted with each other in Spanish, and I understood every word.

I grinned, *very* glad Virginia didn't understand what they were saying.

Chapter 3

I nearly choked trying to keep my giggles inside. Nila and Luisa were sharing their opinions about the young *señorita's* choice of apparel. They were laughing, and pretty soon I would be joining them. It was time to get upstairs.

Nila's dark-brown eyes twinkled with mirth when I grabbed
Virginia's sleeve and brushed past her. "How will you teach
her anything?" she asked, smiling at me. "I fear she weighs so
much she will not be able to climb up on the *caballo*."

I shrugged to show her I had the situation under control, but
I didn't trust myself to speak, not even in Spanish. I hurried
Virginia up the steps, down the hall, and into my room.

Thirty long minutes later, I was teaching Virginia how to
saddle her horse. She looked a sight, but I was breathing easier
now that her corset had been loosened (she refused to take it
off) and she was clad in my split skirt.

It had taken some time to convince Virginia that wearing my
split skirt would not send her down the path to social destruc-
tion. True, no polite ladies wore these newfangled getups; not
even Melinda liked them much.

But I thanked the good Lord every day that Mother had a
practical streak in her that often overruled many of the stuffy
social rules of the day. She would rather have me alive and
unfashionable than stylish and hurt. *Hurrah for Mother!*

When I told Virginia she could run along home if she didn't
want to change her clothes, she grumbled and gave in. Her
ruffled, white blouse and velvet riding hat didn't go with the
dark-brown skirt, but Pal didn't act like he noticed her terrible
fashion statement. She had refused to trade her slippers for a
pair of good, sturdy boots but I let that go.

Virginia was taller than I. My riding skirt fell just below her
knees. She looked stricken that somebody on our ranch might
see her legs.

I laughed. "The only time our ranch hands look at a leg is when
they're tending a lame horse. Your legs are safe as safe can be."

Virginia narrowed her eyes at my joke. I quickly went back
to saddling Taffy.

I didn't want an audience for our lesson, and I was pretty sure

Virginia wanted one even less. The entire ranch was aware of Virginia's recent experience on Pal, when she'd taken off across the yard screaming. Falling head over heels into Whirlwind's corral was her ultimate humiliation.

The men had told and retold the story many times. If they saw Virginia today they were sure to stop whatever they were doing and watch with wide smiles to see what she would do next.

The Circle C ranch hands were a lively crew, but their jokes could be rough and thoughtless. It would be funny, but I would not give them a reason to laugh at Virginia. I determined to find a place where she could learn to ride in peace.

The only really private spot I knew was my special spot up by the creek. By this time of year, the creek was most likely a trickle. Since we weren't going fishing, that didn't pose a problem.

"Come on, Virginia," I coaxed. "Get your foot in the stirrup. I'll do the rest."

Grunting and groaning, Virginia shoved her slippered foot into the stirrup. I gave her backside a hefty shove and she plopped into Pal's saddle. Her fingers turned white clutching the saddle horn.

Pal's ears flicked back, but I quieted him with a gentle command. The last time Virginia rode Pal, she wouldn't let me get up with her. This time I didn't ask. I hauled myself up and squeezed into the saddle behind her.

"I'm smashed!" she protested. "You said you'd teach me to ride. This isn't teaching me anything."

"Be patient," I said. "Do you want every cowhand on the Circle C to watch?"

She shook her head.

"Well then, we have to get away from here. The only way I can figure how to do that is if we ride double. All right?"

I took Virginia's tiny nod as agreement and reached around her middle to unwind the reins from the saddle horn. Gripping them tightly, I turned and whistled for Taffy. She'd follow us all the way to the creek.

Pal seemed nervous, and no wonder. Virginia looked wound up tighter than a spring. "The first thing you need to do is relax," I told her.

Virginia's shoulders sagged about an inch, no more. I prodded Pal in the sides, and Virginia yelped. Maybe she was remembering the last time somebody had kicked Pal.

"Stop hollering," I said.

Pal's trot was enough to jiggle anybody, so I urged him faster. As soon as he broke into a smooth lope, Virginia quieted down. Her fingers turned less white on the horn, but she didn't let go.

The grass was golden brown at my special spot. I slowed Pal and brought him to a stop. Then I slid from his back under the shade of my favorite oak tree.

"Stay on Pal," I said when it looked like Virginia might dismount. I handed her the reins, which she took with one hand. The other hand never left the saddle horn. "Virginia," I said, "you need to relax. Sit up and let go of the saddle horn. Pal's not going anywhere. Not until you tell him to."

Little by little, Virginia began to relax. I couldn't help but think that her last experience on Pal must have really frightened her. She'd seemed much more confident a month ago, the first time she sat on Pal.

"See?" I said. "Pal is happy to let you on his back. Now tighten the reins a bit, lower your hands, sit back, and say, 'walk on.' You can give him a little nudge too."

Virginia looked doubtful, but Pal behaved beautifully, just like I knew he would. He stopped when his rider pulled back gently on the reins, and he walked when she told him to. In no time, she was turning Pal in figure eights. I had to admit that she had a good seat when she wasn't acting terrified. I told her so.

Virginia beamed at my compliment.

I trailed along on foot beside Pal, ready to grab his bridle if Virginia did anything unexpected. "Hold up," I said when I'd had enough of that. "I'm going to mount Taffy. We can ride together."

Virginia nodded. She looked pleased as punch to be walking Pal at a snail's pace. "Why, this is incredibly easy," she said ten minutes later. We had walked up and down alongside the muddy creek bank.

"As long as you're patient and don't get cocky." I looked up at the sky. It was almost noon. I had spent two long hours with Virginia, and she now knew how to walk her horse. "Your first lesson is over," I said. "There's lemonade and sugar cookies back at the house."

Virginia frowned. "What do you mean? We've barely begun. I'm ready for the next step. I would like to trot."

"Not today." I reached out to snag Pal's reins.

Virginia turned his head. "I don't want to go back. I'm just beginning to have fun."

"Virginia!" I was hot, sweaty, and tired of looking after a greenhorn. "We're going back. *Now.*"

Virginia pouted for a few more minutes, then she let out a long, disgusted breath. "Fine," she snipped.

I relaxed. I had a feeling Virginia knew there would be no more lessons if she started acting like a spoiled brat. I was doing her a big favor. It was up to her to play by my rules.

Rule number one: quit while you're ahead.

So far, Virginia had not been hurt. She had not fallen off Pal. Pal had not run away with her. It was the perfect end to a good first lesson.

Virginia shook her head when I offered to take Pal's reins. "I want to walk him back to the ranch myself."

That would take a while, but I resigned myself to the fact that at least we were headed in the right direction. I took the lead and pointed Taffy's nose for home.

That's when I saw them: a couple dozen horses galloping over the rise ahead of us—coming our way. I couldn't see if they were mounted or if they were a group of wild mustangs.

I only knew they were headed straight for us.

Chapter 4

Virginia saw the horses the same instant I did. She squealed in terror. When afraid, I always figure a person's first reaction is to flee the danger. For Virginia, it was just the opposite. She sat frozen in place, with her mouth gaping and her eyes wide and scared.

Pal, on the other hand, was turning in circles, clearly waiting for his rider to give him instructions. If she didn't, it looked like Pal would take matters into his own hooves. He'd run, with or without Virginia's say-so.

I didn't blame him. Taffy was acting skittish and looked ready to bolt. Thundering hooves coming at me made me want to give Taffy her head and get out of there. If I'd been alone, that's exactly what I would have done.

But I didn't have the luxury of saving just my own skin. Before Pal got it into his head to run away, I leaned over and grabbed his reins, ripping them out of Virginia's shaking hands. "Remember when I told you not to hang on to the saddle horn?" I shouted.

She nodded, too terrified to reply.

"Well, forget all that. Grab the saddle horn and hang on for your life!"

With one hand, I gripped Pal's reins. My other hand locked

around Taffy's reins. I didn't want Virginia to see, but my hands were shaking as much as hers. I secured my feet in the stirrups and slammed them against my mare's sides. "Let's go!" I hollered.

Taffy took off like a shot. My arm felt nearly ripped out of my shoulder until Pal decided he was coming along. Virginia screamed, but I ignored her. As long as I could hear her yelling, I knew she was still on Pal.

On we raced. My goal was the open field ahead, where we could swerve and give way to the herd of horses pounding behind us. My greatest fear was being caught up in their stampede, carried along to wherever they happened to be headed. That could be deadly, especially if one of us fell off in the scuffle.

The ground trembled when the horses drew near. Taffy could have outrun them, but Pal couldn't keep up. We were being overtaken. My heart hammered inside my chest. *Hurry, hurry!* I urged Taffy. Virginia was still screaming.

We made it to the clearing. I yanked Taffy hard to the left and she turned immediately. Pal galloped right behind her. I chanced a quick glance behind my shoulder. Thankfully, Virginia was still with me. She'd lost her fancy velvet hat, and her long, pale hair blew in all directions.

I wanted to slow down, but I didn't dare. *Please keep going the other way!* I mentally screamed at the stampeding horses. They didn't. They turned with us, as if wanting to catch Taffy and Pal up in their wild chase.

Suddenly, a huge, gray blur flashed past us. I gasped. *Whirlwind?*

It couldn't be, yet here he was. Chad's maverick stallion was up to his old tricks, trying to gather up all the horses on the ranch. He nipped at Taffy as he raced by. Taffy whinnied her distress and kicked out her hind legs but kept her pace.

Pal suddenly shied to the left and reared midflight. *Snap!* The reins yanked from my hands. "Hang on, Virginia!" I screamed over the roaring in my ears. "Don't let go no matter what!"

Right then I was glad I had convinced Virginia to shed her riding habit for my more practical split skirt. She had abandoned the saddle horn and was gripping Pal, both arms encircling his neck. Free at last, Pal joined the band of horses and headed across the range.

Fear clutched my belly. Taffy and I had been left behind, but Virginia was off on a riding adventure that could easily end in tragedy. "Please, God, don't let her fall off," I prayed. I had never meant for anything like this to happen. I'd done everything slowly, with Virginia's safety in mind. Yet it was dissolving into a disaster.

"What do I do?" I hollered at the horses' back ends. I'd urged Taffy to follow the herd, and she was gaining on them. But what could I do even if I caught up? I saw the pale streak of Virginia's hair flying behind her like a horse's mane. Pal blended into the herd. If Virginia was still screaming, I couldn't hear it above the noise of the horses' pounding hooves and snorting.

There was no escape. They might run for the next hour and end up clear at the Kings River. Those dumb horses sure weren't headed for the ranch. I clenched my jaw, tightened my grip on Taffy's reins, and pressed her even faster.

From the corner of my eye I spotted a horse and rider gallop up and pass me far to the left. A rider? Here? Now? He raced by so quickly I couldn't make out who it was at first. Then I recognized the horse. It was Mitch on Chase—the fastest horse on our ranch.

Were Mitch and Chase fast enough to catch up to Virginia? Even if they could, how would Mitch squeeze between the wildly racing horses without killing himself? I slowed Taffy and started praying with all my might. Mitch had rushed by without acknowledging I was there. It looked as if his gaze was glued on Virginia. She was hard to miss, even in the dust.

Slowly—too slowly it seemed to me—Chase and Mitch caught up with the herd. I watched him wedge Chase into the middle of the fray, and I prayed harder. I needn't have worried. Ten seconds later, Mitch had scooped Virginia off Pal and was carrying her across his saddle, away from the runaway herd.

As soon as he and Virginia were free from danger, Mitch slowed down and walked Chase back to where I sat on Taffy. I was shaking. Sweat poured down my face in little rivulets. Or were they tears? When I caught myself sobbing, I knew I was blubbering bucketsful.

I didn't care. "Is she all r-right?" I stammered.

Mitch didn't answer. His face was white.

I steeled myself for some big-brother yelling.

Chapter 5

Mitch did not yell. He brought Chase to a stop, slid from the saddle, and gently lowered Virginia into his arms. "She's right as rain," he said.

Virginia wasn't sobbing like I was. Her cries came in little hiccups, and she was trembling. But she didn't faint.

Here was Virginia, terrified beyond all reason, inches from death, and she hadn't swooned. In fact, she wasn't doing anything but lying limply in Mitch's arms. When he attempted to lower her to the ground, she whimpered, so he hefted her up higher.

"It's all right, Miss Foster," he said in his most gentlemanly tone. "I've got you."

Virginia shed more tears and clutched Mitch's vest.

"Shh," Mitch consoled her. "You're going to be fine, just as soon as I get you back to the house."

The house. Mother. Mrs. Foster.

I gulped. Somehow I knew this was going to be looked on as my fault.

"Why didn't you stay in the yard?" Mother would ask.

"Why did I ever trust you?" Mrs. Foster would wail.

They were right. I should not have left the yard. I should not have worried about the ranch hands watching. Too many things can go wrong out on the range—the unexpected herd of runaways for one thing. No doubt they were on a jaunt and having a grand time. But Whirlwind, seeing a couple more horses on the horizon, would naturally want to nab them as his own.

Mitch spoke up. "That maverick's going to be the death of somebody one of these days. Chad should just shoot him." He frowned and watched the horizon, where a puff of dust showed the herd's passing. "I hope Pal's got sense enough to leave that herd eventually and come home."

"Maybe his saddle will chafe him and drive him back to the barn," I offered, swiping at my eyes. I didn't look at Virginia. I was too ashamed. This was all my fault.

"Hey, sis," Mitch said. "Don't take it so hard. You're safe.

Virginia's safe. I was tracking that herd most of the morning, trying to see what Whirlwind was up to. He's a useless hunk of horsemeat, and Chad's going to hear about it from me."

I nodded, numb. My heart thumped. What would happen when we returned home? I looked at the ground. "I'm sorry, Virginia. I surely didn't mean for this to happen." I really *was* sorry. I felt terrible.

Then Virginia surprised me. Actually, she shocked me. "All's well that ends well," she said, smiling. Her gray eyes glistened with tears, and her voice was shaky.

My head snapped up at her words. "Do you mean that?"

Virginia nodded. "I stayed on the horse, didn't I?"

"You sure did!" Mitch and I said at the same time.

"You're a grand rider," I added, "for a first lesson."

"I bet Andi couldn't have done better," Mitch put in.

I frowned. That was taking things too far. I bit my tongue when Mitch winked at me.

"When I told you to let go," Mitch said, "you obeyed instantly. Good girl."

Virginia glowed under his praise. Or was it something more? She was looking at Mitch with adoration. Well, why not? My brother probably saved her life. Why wouldn't she be grateful?

"You saved me," she said, tearing up once more. "I know this wasn't Andi's fault. It was that awful—what's his name?—Whirlwind's fault. You rescued me in the nick of time." She fluttered her eyelashes at Mitch. "It was probably the most exhilarating moment of my life when you pulled me off Pal and onto your horse."

When Virginia ducked her head and sighed, Mitch rolled his eyes at me.

I muffled my giggles.

"Please don't tell my mother about my near-death experience," Virginia murmured. "She will never let me ride another horse." She lifted her gaze to Mitch's suntanned face. "And I *do* so look forward to my next lesson."

"Next lesson?" I was stunned she wanted to go anywhere near another horse.

"Oh, yes. I can't wait until next Saturday."

By now, Mitch had lifted Virginia back on his horse and had mounted up behind her. I scrambled up on Taffy and prodded her forward.

Virginia gave me a wide smile. Then she tilted her head back and glanced up at Mitch. "I was wondering . . ." She paused. "Would you be willing to help Andi with my next lesson? I feel so safe when I'm with you."

Mitch looked bewildered.

Poor Mitch! But I didn't feel sorry enough for him to stick around. I dug my heels into Taffy's sides and plunged ahead. I didn't want Virginia—or Mitch—to hear the gales of laughter that burst out as I hightailed it back to the ranch.

10

Where the Trees Meet the Bay

July 1881
This story takes place not long after Andrea Carter and the
Trouble with Treasure.

Chapter 1

Water. Lots of it. Everywhere I looked. A spray of icy-cold
Puget Sound slapped my cheeks and I gasped.

"Crazy, that's what I am," I chided myself under my breath.
"Plumb *loco*."

Why would I trade the hot summer days in Central California, where winter rains were months away, to journey to a
chunk of wilderness hundreds of miles north in Washington
Territory?

A telegram from Jenny Grant had started it all . . .

My friend from Miss Whitaker's Academy telegraphed to
let me know she'd made it home safely after her visit to the
Circle C. Then she begged me to come and see her before
school started in the fall.

I stood in the doorway, stunned at the invitation. The mes-
senger boy, generous tip in hand, had ridden off several minutes before.

Mitch peeked over my shoulder and whistled. "That wire must have cost Jenny's father a pretty penny."

True, the two-page telegram read more like a letter, but Jenny's father could afford it. He was a rich lumberman in a territory that grew trees thicker than a valley rancher could grow wheat.

FAIR'S FAIR, the telegram had ended.

I didn't think Mother would let me go, but when I half-heartedly asked her, she shocked me with her answer.

"You have been through a lot this past month." She glanced at Mitch, who was still hobbling around. His shot-up leg was healing, but slowly. "I think getting away from the ranch and the upheaval would be good for you."

"B-but, Mother," I stammered. "Taffy's in foal and I ought not to leave her. Besides, I—"

"Don't you want to go?" Mother asked, eyebrows raised. "I know you and Jenny talked about it."

Sure we had. But that's all I thought it was . . . talk.

Mother was still speaking. "You could escape the heat and widen your horizons at the same time. You'd be away no more than a month or six weeks. The larger steamers can churn up and down the coast in a matter of days."

I was caught in my own trap. Before she boarded the train to Oakland and the bay, I'd told Jenny I'd love to visit Washington Territory someday.

I never dreamed "someday" would come so soon.

"If you decline the opportunity, you'll have to wait another year," Mother finished. "By then you'll have a foal to train and—"

"I know." I let the telegram drop to a small table in the foyer. "I think I would like to go." I said it before I changed my mind.

Nobody in my family would ever learn I was a coward. I had hated water ever since I'd nearly drowned last November. The thought of steaming north through the endless Pacific Ocean with the safe, dry coastline out of reach terrified me.

Mother smiled. "I'll make the arrangements."

◆ ◆ ◆

That's how I found myself with water in my eyes and hair, paddlewheels sloshing night and day, and a heavy cloud cover most of the trip.

The friendly captain found me sitting on deck the morning before we were to make port. "Lass, it won't be long now. Tacoma will be in our sights by mid-afternoon."

I strained my eyes to see through the gray haze. It wasn't fog exactly, more like a constant, light drizzle. "How can you tell?" I asked. "Maybe we'll steam right past the dock."

Captain Donahue laughed. "Nay, lass. The clouds will break up by this afternoon."

I was not convinced.

I felt damp and chilled up on deck, but staying in my cabin was worse. It was decent enough, and the food was pretty good. But the *Yosemite* made the trip to Washington Territory twice a month. She was designed for speed, not comfort.

Worse, the companion Mother found to accompany me ended up seasick most of the trip. She turned out to be useless as a chaperone. I didn't want her telling Mother tales, so I stayed in her company as much as I could stand. I slipped away for fresh air on deck whenever she napped—usually after an encounter with a bucket.

The stinking results of seasickness cannot be overstated.

Thankfully, Captain Donahue noticed my plight and took me under his wing. He treated me with all respect and shared stories of his daughter Ruth, who lived in Seattle. The captain also knew Jenny Grant's family and spoke highly of them.

As a result, I ended up with the run of the ship under the captain's watchful eye whenever Mrs. Johansen was asleep—which was often. I was grateful but wary. After all, there was all that cold water everywhere I looked.

Mrs. Johansen left the *Yosemite* in Port Townsend. I had a day and a half of total freedom after that. Perhaps if the captain had given me permission to wear sailors' duds and put me to work, I would not have had time to fret over the closeness of the sea.

As it was, I spent a lot of time up in the pilothouse, where I saw plenty of water. And clouds. And occasionally a long, unbroken band of green in the distance.

Chapter 2

Captain Donahue's weather prediction proved true. Along about three o'clock that afternoon, the clouds dissolved. First a streak of sky appeared, then more, until finally the entire sky turned into a blue canopy.

Where the clouds went, I had no idea. They were there one minute but vanished the next.

"Summer on the Sound," the captain explained.

That didn't explain anything to my mind, but I smiled politely and turned my face eastward, where the coastline was drawing nearer. The last several damp, cloudy days had transformed into a warm, crystal-clear summer afternoon. Out here on the water, the breeze turned gentle and kept me cool.

Beauty and color exploded before my eyes. Instead of slate-gray, the water had turned a deep blue-green. A thousand diamonds sparkled on the waves. Dozens of seagulls bobbed up and down with the current, floating past the steamer without a care in the world.

The water raced to meet the green, green shore. I never dreamed there could be so many evergreen trees in the whole world. They grew thicker than carrots. Rising high above the trees and small hills, a towering, snowcapped peak came into view.

"What'd you think of Mount Rainier?" the captain asked. "She's a beauty, ain't she?"

"She sure is," I agreed.

"There's Tacoma." Captain Donahue pointed to a finger of land sticking out into the Sound. "It ain't Seattle, but they do all right."

Buildings of all shapes and sizes came into view. Tall-masted sailing ships and steamers, along with tugboats and barges, busily made their way in and out of the harbor.

By the time the *Yosemite* blew her whistle, I had packed my carpetbags and hauled my luggage up on deck. I wanted to be the first person off this boat.

"Andi!" a shrill voice rose above the babble of deckhands preparing to dock. Not fifty feet away, Jenny stood waving her hands above her head and jumping up and down like a marionette.

I waved back. Then . . . *clunk!*

The *Yosemite* hit the dock and I nearly fell overboard. I caught myself just in time. I was itchy to disembark. The captain let me go down the narrow gangplank first. "The crew will tote your bags," he said. "Go on with ya now, lass." He chuckled.

Dry land at last!

Jenny and I collided, throwing our arms around each other in happy abandon. Out of breath, she introduced me to her little brother, Gideon, and her nearest brother in age, Micah.

Jenny had three more older brothers, but they were nowhere in sight. I wouldn't have remembered their names anyway. She talked a mile a minute as she pulled me along.

"And here's my mama and papa," she said, shoving her wild cascade of red tangles back from her face.

"How do you do, Miss Carter?" Mrs. Grant said, taking my hand. In spite of the mud everywhere—especially around the docks—Jenny's mother seemed right at home. My mother could maintain an air of elegance in the middle of a cattle drive. Mrs. Grant looked like she could match her.

"We're honored you could come for a visit," Jenny's father said.

He was tall, even taller than Chad, who easily hits six feet. Mr. Grant's hair was auburn, and he sported an auburn mustache and beard. Instead of a suit, he wore lumberjack clothes with suspenders and high, laced boots.

I liked him at once.

"Micah, Gideon, take her baggage up to the house," Mr. Grant said. He pointed to where a sailor had dropped my carpetbags near the gangplank.

The two boys hopped to it. They started fighting over who could carry it the fastest then vanished around a corner. Would I ever see my luggage again?

Jenny didn't give me time to worry about it. She clasped my hand and off we went. Where to, I had no idea. She didn't bid her parents good-bye or tell them where we were going. She just ran, dragging me along beside her.

"You'll be more comfortable once you get out of that stiff traveling getup," Jenny said.

I opened my mouth to speak then quickly shut it.

"Don't worry if you didn't bring your casual clothes. I've got plenty. We can snag a pair of Micah's britches if we need to." She shrugged. "You'll have to roll up the cuffs, but I think they'll fit otherwise."

Jenny was wearing a dress, clearly not by choice. It hung crooked and rumpled. By the time we slammed onto the back porch of her two-story, white clapboard home, the front of her dress was mud-splattered.

I was splattered too, in spite of the now-sunny skies.

"Better get used to it," Jenny said, laughing at the look on my face. "It rains a lot here. What do you think grows good trees? I'm hopin' the skies stay clear for a few days. I've got plenty to show you. We'll have a jim-dandy time."

I had no doubt about that.

Chapter 3

For three days, Jenny took me on a whirlwind tour of Tacoma: the docks, the sawmills, and the miles and miles of forests and beaches.

The fourth day, Jenny, Micah, Gideon, and I mounted horses and rode out to an unused military reservation called Point Defiance. It was the finger of land the captain had pointed out when we were steaming into Tacoma.

I marveled at the freedom Jenny and her brothers had. I was ready to ask her about it when I remembered how far from home Cory and I roamed on the ranch. Somehow, though, open range seemed a lot friendlier than the rough, narrow bridle paths through hundreds of acres of dark woods.

The forest of Point Defiance opened up onto the bay. There were trees, then there was water. A narrow strip of rocks and sand separated the trees from the water at high tide.

I stayed far away from the beach. All that cold, deep water made me shudder.

The next day turned hot. A nice breeze blew across the water and into town, but Jenny—always one to complain about the heat—suggested we go bathing.

"*What?*"

"Bathing in the Sound," Jenny said. She pulled her oldest dress over her bloomers, tied back her hair, and grinned.

I stood in her room unmoving. "I don't bathe in salt water."

"Just try it," Jenny insisted. "Put a toe in. We can catch mud crabs and collect kelp."

"Kelp makes bully-good whips," Gideon piped up from outside Jenny's door. "Hurry up, slowpokes!"

I sighed and halfheartedly pulled on a pair of overalls Micah had tossed my way the day before. Britches would protect me from the cold water better than a thin, calico dress over my under-drawers. "All right, Jenny," I said. "One toe in the water. And catching crabs might be fun."

It was! The tide was out down by the docks. Every time Gideon turned over a barnacle-encrusted rock, dozens of tiny, hard-shelled creatures scurried to find holes in the mud.

Most of the crabs were no bigger than my thumb. Their tiny claws tried to pinch my hand, but it only tickled. Then Gideon found a big one, at least an inch and a half across. He held up a stick, where the helpless crab dangled by one claw—a *big* claw.

"Almost eating size," the little boy teased.

I bent close to get a better look. That crab looked so angry! It foamed at the mouth and waved its free claw around, pinching the air.

Then *plop!* The crab let go and fell to the mudflats. It scurried under a rock before Gideon could catch him. The rock was too big to move.

"Oh, clamshells!" he yelled. A minute later, Gideon forgot about the crabs. He yanked a slimy, green, seaweed-type plant off the rocks and started popping the air bladders. Next, he coiled a long rope of kelp.

"Now I'm a stage driver!" he called out, snapping his "whip." The bulb end of the kelp made a good handle.

Before long, Jenny and I joined him. We whacked each other with kelp until I was laughing so hard I had to stop and rest.

Slowly, the tide crept in. The rocks and mud crabs became

covered with a layer of foamy, icy water. I stuck my toe in. Puget Sound was the coldest water I'd ever felt. Even the winter-cold creek I'd fallen into last November did not compare to this.

To my amazement, Jenny plunged into the water and ducked her whole head under. Then she burst to the surface, shivering. "It's refreshing!" she said. "Come on in. Try it!"

Gideon ran in, splashing. Soon, brother and sister were engaged in an all-out water fight. I watched from the shore. I stood barefoot in four inches of water and watched it lap around my quickly numbing feet. When the water got deeper, I backed up.

Those two crazy Grant kids kept at it for at least twenty minutes. When their faces turned blue and gooseflesh covered their bodies, they left the water and fell to the sandy beach next to where I now sat.

"You missed some fun," Jenny said. Her teeth chattered.

"That's all right," I said. "I had more fun watching."

The July sun quickly dried Jenny and Gideon. We sat on the beach, wiggling our toes in the hot sand and looking for agates—small, see-through pebbles.

When the tide grew higher, Gideon looked at Jenny and said, "It's time."

Chapter 4

Jenny dropped her agates in her dress pocket and stood up. Shaking off the sand, she reached down to grab my hand.

"Where are we going?" I rose slowly, not sure what new adventure Jenny and her little brother had in mind. I was game, though, as long as it had nothing to do with water.

I should have known better.

"We're going crabbing off the dock," Gideon said. "It's nigh on high tide."

I looked out over the shoreline. The rocks where the mud crabs hid were covered with water.

"Not mud crabs," Jenny said, giggling at my ignorance. "Dungeness crabs. The eating kind. We catch 'em, boil 'em right on the beach, crack 'em, and eat 'em."

Gideon rubbed his stomach. "Good eating, crab."

The vision of those little mud crabs ten times their size terrified me. "You eat those things?" I asked, aghast.

"You bet!" Gideon said.

Jenny laughed. "Don't look so shocked, Andi. You eat rattlesnake. We eat crab."

Jenny had a point. I shrugged and kept quiet.

They dragged me along the shoreline to a narrow pier. It stretched probably fifty feet over the water, out into the bay. Near the shore side of the dock lay a coil of rope and a contraption that looked like a cross between a barrel and a leaky crate. Jenny and Gideon heaved it up and started dragging it onto the pier.

I tagged along, curious.

Jenny and Gideon worked like a well-matched team. I stood at the end of the pier and looked down into the deep, dark water. I then looked around for other people. A few were fishing off another pier, but this one was deserted.

If someone fell off the dock at high tide, he'd be a goner. I marveled once again at the Grants' freedom before common sense took over. It was no more dangerous than riding a horse around in the middle of nowhere.

I relaxed.

Jenny and Gideon were struggling with something inside the barrel. The smell told me that whatever it was had seen better days. I glanced down. "Ew! Fish heads! What are they for?"

"We secure them in the barrel," Jenny explained. "Crabs love fish heads—"

"And raw chicken parts," Gideon chimed in.

"We drop the barrel off the end of the pier," Jenny continued. "It falls over on its side on the bottom. The fish-head smell brings the crabs. They climb into the trap to get the fish."

She plugged her nose. "With any luck, we pull up the crab pot before they escape. It shouldn't take long. These fish heads are really ripe."

With that, the Grant kids lowered the makeshift crab trap into the water. Slowly, they let the line out until it went slack.

"Now we wait," Gideon said. He tied the end of the rope around the nearest piling.

For the next twenty minutes, we sat on the end of the dock, swinging our feet and talking. The sun blazed down. It felt almost as hot as California.

Then Jenny stood up. "I'm going up to the house for something to eat and drink. I'll be back in a jiffy with food for us all. You two stay here and guard our pot." Her eyebrows came together. "I don't want any poachers stealing our crabs."

She ran down the length of the pier and out of sight.

Gideon and I sat side by side for a few minutes. I liked him. Jenny's little brother reminded me of my nephew, Levi, but without the rough edges. Gideon had red curls and a face full of freckles. I could tell he adored his big sister.

"Let's take a peek at our catch," he said suddenly.

"Huh?"

"Pull it up and see what we've got so far." He jumped to his feet and grabbed a length of the rope. The end was still tied around the piling.

"We should wait for Jenny." I wasn't excited about taking giant-sized crabs with waving pincers out of a rickety-looking trap and putting them in a tub of bay water. I envisioned missing fingers. *My* missing fingers.

"I'll grab the crabs," Gideon said as if he could read my mind. "You just help me pull up the crab pot."

Easier said than done. The heavy, wooden barrel didn't budge. I yanked harder; Gideon yanked. It moved up a few feet, but I was panting.

"Pull harder!" Gideon said. He planted his feet near the edge of the pier, took a deep breath, and pulled.

Just then my fingers slipped. My hands slid along the rope, burning them. I let go.

The crab pot plunged down. With a yelp, Gideon tripped and flew off the dock. As he fell, his head hit the edge of the pier. Then he dropped like a rock into the water.

Chapter 5

My heart froze. My burning hands turned cold. I ran to the edge of the dock. "Gideon!" I whipped my head around and screamed. "Jenny! Anybody!"

No response. The fishermen were too far away to hear me over the breaking waves and the seagulls' cries.

Gideon's head popped up to the surface. He took a breath. I lay flat on my stomach and reached out as far as I could. "Grab my hand!"

The little boy looked at me, confused. Then his eyes rolled back in his head and he slumped. The water covered him.

"No!" I shrieked. Gideon was going to drown! What could I do?

The answer hit like a bucket of ice water. *Go after him.*

I shrank back. "I can't. I can't. I—"

Before I talked myself out of entering that dark water, I twisted around on my stomach and let my legs and feet hang over the pier. "Help me save him, Jesus, because you know how scared I am."

I let myself drop into icy Puget Sound. I couldn't swim well, so I grabbed the first lifeline I found—a piling. There were plenty to choose from. They held up the dock and were spaced about every six feet or so to the shore. I hugged it and slid farther into the water.

The freezing water took my breath away. My legs and feet went numb. It was just as well. The barnacles on the piling scraped my bare lower legs. I'd rolled up the overalls earlier that day, and now I was paying the price.

A wave surged and caught me in the face. Salt water flooded my nose and mouth. I coughed and gagged.

The wave brought Gideon close. With one hand firmly grasped around the thick piling, I snatched at the floating boy.

My hand caught him by the hair, and I yanked his head out of the water.

It seemed longer, but barely a minute had passed between Gideon going senseless and my drop into the bay. "G-Gideon," I stammered. My teeth chattered. "Wake up. We g-gotta get outta the water."

Gideon's eyes remained closed. A long, deep gash cut across his forehead and dripped blood.

I caught my breath and held it. Panic was only seconds away. *Keep me calm, God*, I prayed. I didn't know what to do. *Show me what to do.*

We couldn't stay here under the pier, not with the tide nearly high. I looked up. The dock was only a foot above my head, but I could barely lift myself out of the water, much less the limp little boy I was clutching. I had him around the armpits.

I wasn't going anywhere.

Another wave slapped me in the face, trying to push me away from the piling. I held tighter and looked around. Not far away another piling loomed. Maybe, just maybe . . .

When the next surge came, I was ready. I kicked away from the piling and let the surge carry me toward the next one. Gideon and I both went under.

I felt for the piling and pulled myself and Gideon out of the water. Now I was really shivering. Gideon lay still. His head lolled against my shoulder.

I was wet and cold, but I was a little closer to shore. I knew what to do the next time. The next three pilings were easier to grab, but I was shaking uncontrollably. I nearly lost my grip on Gideon.

The shore was now no more than twenty feet away. I kicked off for the next piling and got a surprise. My bare feet scraped along slippery, seaweed-covered rocks. I was touching bottom!

I don't remember what happened next. One minute I was

slipping and sliding toward shore. I kept Gideon's head above water and dragged him along next to me. The next minute I was on shore, collapsing onto the warm sand and breathing a thank-you to God and to whomever had yanked Gideon and me the last few yards.

* * *

After fishing us out of the water, Mr. and Mrs. Grant made sure I was wrapped up in a blanket. They tended the multiple barnacle scrapes on my legs. I sat on the beach in the sand and gloried in the fact that Jenny's little brother was alive.

Gideon had not been in the water long enough to get water in his lungs, but he'd apparently swallowed a lot of it. When he came to, he immediately threw up, crying and choking. "My head hurts," he sobbed. He looked around. "Who's watching the crab pot?"

Everybody laughed. Mr. Grant and his oldest son, Eli, went to pull up the pot. When they showed us the catch and heard how Gideon had gone overboard, Mr. Grant shook his head. "No wonder," he said. "The number and size of these crabs is astonishing. That pot was so heavy that Eli and I could hardly manage it."

The crab feast was wonderful. "I like crab," I said after cracking and eating both claws of a monster crab. He must have been ten inches across his back.

The rest of my visit stayed quiet. But I discovered something else after that day. I wasn't afraid of the water anymore. When Jenny rose to cool off after a long rest in the hot sand, I shouted, "Hey! Wait for me!" and took off after her.

II

Adiós, Jeffrey Sullivan

August 1881
This story takes place just before the events in Andrea Carter and the
Price of Truth.

Chapter 1

I always thought Melinda was blind to the faults of her beau,
Jeffrey Sullivan. From the time he began courting her, I had a
funny feeling about his intentions.

I don't know why I felt that way. Jeffrey was not rude, nor
was he a bully like Johnny Wilson. Jeffrey was always polite, at
least in front of my family. I tried not to ever see him alone. I
think he suspected I didn't like him much.

Jeffrey always dressed like he had the town by the tail. He
wore fancy white shirts with ruffles (I heard him tell Melinda
his clothes came straight from Paris) and a high collar.

"It's all the rage," he insisted when I snickered.

His collar looked tight enough to choke him. On the top of
his blond waves, he usually wore a tall hat like grown-up men
do in the city.

"He only wears it to look taller," I told Melinda once. "And
he has *shifty eyes!*"

She slammed her bedroom door after telling me I'd better leave Jeffrey alone. "He's kind, considerate, and very attentive," she shouted through the door. "Not to mention handsome."

You need to step out of your dream world, big sister. I didn't say it out loud. I didn't want another door slammed in my face.

"Just think, he might become my brother-in-law someday," I moaned to Taffy every time I heard Jeffrey's name. "I'm sure he glares at me because he knows that *I* know he isn't who he pretends to be. He puts on fancy airs and squires Melinda to dances and box socials. She giggles and thinks he's simply the *nicest* gentleman."

Taffy snorted and laid her ears back. That told me she had Jeffrey figured out too.

Jeffrey's family is as nice as they can be. I love his little sister Emily. I catch butterflies for her or turn the jump rope at recess for her and her little friends. Their father, Mr. Sullivan, is the town's druggist and owns the apothecary shop.

Nice family or not, I could not push aside the creepy feeling that hit me every time I saw Mr. Jeffrey Sullivan. My thoughts were uncharitable, but I was sure he liked Melinda because he thinks, and rightly so, that our family has a lot of money. The best way to get himself a piece of the Carter pie was by marrying Melinda.

My anxious thoughts finally took me to Justin. I confided in him, and he laughed. Then he got serious and told me to mind my own business and leave Melinda alone.

If I were convinced Jeffrey loved Melinda with all his heart, I would have done what Justin told me. But not one week after Justin's talk, something made me loathe that sneaky fellow more than ever. I knew somebody had to rescue Melinda from Jeffrey Sullivan's clutches.

I was happy to take on the job.

♦ ♦ ♦

On that dreadful day, Mother asked me to ride into town and pick up some potions and medicines at the drugstore. I saddled Taffy and enjoyed a brisk ride along the valley road. When I arrived in Fresno, I looped the reins around the hitching post and hopped up onto the boardwalk. I was just reaching for the doorknob to Sullivan's Apothecary when I heard a strange noise. It sounded like giggling and a couple of low-pitched voices.

Being naturally curious, I tiptoed along the building front and poked my head around the corner. A fellow and a girl were talking together in the alley. *Dumb place to chat*, I thought to myself.

Then the fellow turned his head slightly. I clapped a hand over my mouth to keep from yelping. It was that *rat*, Jeffrey Sullivan, and Libby Flanders. Together. Scandalously close together. I hadn't recognized Jeffrey right away because for once he wasn't wearing his hat.

I recognized Libby, though. Her family runs the Triple L ranch (named for Libby, Laura, and Lana, the Flanders daughters) down by the Kings River. They hardly ever came to town, as Visalia is closer to their spread than Fresno is. But our families see each other once in a while, and Chad knows Ty Flanders, Libby's father, real well.

I jumped back in shock, hoping neither one saw me. Oh, was I ever burning up! I clenched my fists, counted to twenty-five in Spanish then backwards in French (I had learned some French at that girls' school I attended earlier in the year). I tried to "cool my heels" like Justin is always telling me to do. He tells me I jump to conclusions too fast and make snap judgments.

So I took a deep breath and decided that maybe it was just

a friendly chat. I stepped to the corner and peeked again . . . just in time to see Jeffrey give Libby a big kiss right on her lips!

I gasped.

Jeffrey and Libby jumped apart so fast you'd think a bee had stung them. I wish one had. A whole nest of hornets would be just the ticket for that two-timing, girl-chasing rat. I planted my hands on my hips and glared at the guilty parties. "Jeffrey Sullivan, just wait 'til Melinda hears about this!"

How many other rich girls was the druggist's son stringing along? Playing nice to? Pretending to be their beau? *Oooh!* That ungodly, inconsiderate, disloyal beast! I called him worse than that in my head and turned to go.

Chapter 2

I hurried to complete the errand Mother had sent me to town for. My hands shook so much I could hardly open the door to the apothecary.

Just before I stepped inside, Libby Flanders snatched my sleeve. "Wait, Andi."

Liberty is a year younger than Melinda and pretty, with nut-brown eyes, long lashes, and dark, curly hair. Even though she lives on a ranch, she doesn't dress like she belongs there. Not even Melinda dresses as "city" as Libby. Libby loves her big, floppy hats and silk dresses. She's nice enough, but I don't know her very well.

"What are you doing so far from the Triple L?" I asked. I suddenly felt sorry for her. Maybe Libby didn't know Jeffrey was supposed to be keeping company with my big sister. Their courtship had even progressed to the point where Jeffrey had ridden out to the ranch one evening to talk with Mother and Justin about the whole thing.

Obviously, somebody was mixed up about what courtship means, and the confusion wasn't on the Carter side.

I couldn't wait to find Justin and tell him that he, Chad, and Mitch had better do something before Melinda ended up marrying Jeffrey the Rat and bringing disgrace on our whole family.

It was bad enough that my sister Kate had run away and married that disreputable fellow, Troy. But to let Melinda get suckered into Jeffrey's net was more than I could bear. I wanted to protect my sister and unveil Jeffrey's real intentions, which seemed to be to find a rich girl to marry. Apparently it didn't matter which one.

"The whole family came into Fresno today," Libby answered.

I was so upset I'd already forgotten I'd asked a question.

"Father plans to attend a cattle auction at the stockyards," she continued. "Mother and my sisters want to see the new dresses in the emporium." She smiled. "I heard the McLaughlins are hosting a big barn dance this coming Saturday night. Father says we may stay in town and attend. Will you be going?"

I nodded, but I couldn't keep my mind on any dumb barn dance. Not when all I could think of was Jeffrey's horrible behavior.

"So," I said, swallowing. I didn't want to shock her too fast. "How do you know Jeffrey Sullivan?" I didn't include, *And why are you being so friendly with him?*

Libby's expression twisted into a look of confusion, as if she knew nothing. Which she probably didn't. "Mr. Sullivan was in Visalia the other day and we got to know each other," she said. "We were just renewing our acquaintance. Why would Melinda care one way or the other?"

Take a good guess! I wanted to shout.

Before I could spill the news that Jeffrey was Melinda's beau, the Rat rounded the corner and pointed a long, white finger at me. "Finish your business in town and go home."

"This isn't over," I told him.

"Yes, it is," he said. "Go on. Get out of here."

I burst into the drugstore and slammed the door behind me. If Cory or Jack or even Johnny Wilson had bossed me like that, I would have said much, much more. But something deep inside told me this was different. It was serious, not a petty fight with my friends. This was something my brothers had to deal with.

And fast.

Chapter 3

I knew that as soon as my brothers and Melinda heard about this, Jeffrey's education in righteous behavior would begin. The Carter Brothers Justice System is foolproof.

I smiled at the thought.

It didn't take me long to buy the potions Mother wanted. Mr. Sullivan wrapped them carefully in brown paper so they wouldn't break. I tore out of the drugstore, throwing a quick thank-you behind my shoulder. Then I jammed the medicines into my saddlebag and mounted Taffy so fast that she snorted and tossed her head.

"Sorry, girl," I apologized.

My first thought was to rush over to Justin's office, but I'd done that once too often lately.

"No more bursting in on me, young lady," he told me just last week. "I mean it. You are thirteen years old. Unless it's an emergency—and heaven knows you have your share of them— you will wait your turn. I'm happy to take you to lunch or listen to your problems, but *please* make an appointment first."

This was an emergency, but Justin might not agree.

The next best idea was to tell Melinda what her faithless beau was up to. "Yes," I told Taffy. "I might as well go straight to the heart of the matter."

Luckily, Melinda was home instead of off on one of those

Ladies' Aid meetings she loves so much. I spilled what I'd seen and expected Melinda to turn rigid with anger.

She got angry, all right. But first she burst into tears. That was fine with me. She was finally figuring Jeffrey out, something I'd felt in my gut for over a year. I waited for her thanks.

"Shall I get pen and ink so you can write him a nasty letter?" I offered cheerfully. "I'm happy to help you word it. I can deliver it too if you'd like."

Melinda stopped crying and turned on me with all the wrath of an older sister. "Andrea Carter, how dare you! How could you make up such a story? I know you don't like Jeffrey, but to try to break things up like this? Well, it's mean and petty. It hurts and—" She rose from her bed and pointed to the door. "Out. And don't come back until you're ready to apologize."

My mouth dropped open. I was so surprised that I couldn't say a word. Melinda looked angrier than I'd ever seen her before. Not even her fury when I accidentally spilled a jar of spiders in her room compared with this.

I gulped and fled.

She slammed the door so hard behind me that it shook the hallway. Tears stung my eyes, but they were nothing compared to what I heard from behind Melinda's closed door. What hurt most was that she wasn't crying because Jeffrey had betrayed her. No, she was sobbing because she thought I was playing a mean trick on her.

It's true I've played tricks on Melinda, most of them spider- or snake-related, but I would never joke about something as serious as the man she might marry someday. Even *I* know better than that.

I sniffed back my tears and went riding. "I reckon she'll just have to figure it out for herself," I told Taffy. "I'm through helping her. It's over."

Chapter 4

It *wasn't* over. Not by a long shot. By the time I sat down for supper, the whole family had heard Melinda's tale, and she still wasn't speaking to me. Worse, it looked like nobody was ready to believe me.

Justin prayed over the meal. When I opened my eyes I knew I was in hot water. Nobody was smiling. Justin was giving me his will-you-never-learn-to-think-before-you-act look.

My brothers didn't believe me. Neither did Mother. My stomach turned over. I never dreamed my family would turn on me like this. When I tried to bring up the subject, Mother shut me down.

"I'd rather not hear about it, Andrea," she said quietly.

One look at Melinda's red-rimmed eyes told me why. I ducked my head, my appetite gone.

Mitch nudged me. I peeked at him, and he winked. That made me feel a little better, but not much. I knew Mitch didn't think very highly of Jeffrey, but when it came to being in trouble, what Mitch thought didn't really count. Mostly, what *Mother* thought counted, and she was taking Melinda's side.

I expected that soon Mother would insist I apologize, but that I could not do. I was trying to *save* Melinda.

I sat in moody silence while the rest of the family talked about the weather, the hay harvest, and the upcoming barn dance. I nearly choked when Melinda said, "Jeffrey is coming out to the ranch tomorrow to take me for a buggy ride. He just purchased a new rig, with a cover that slides up and down just as slick as you please. If it rains, we won't get wet." She smiled, but it looked forced.

I had the good sense to keep my mouth shut. But I was thinking plenty. *Rain, Melinda? Really? It never rains in August.*

My heart hammered at the thought of Jeffrey's upcoming visit. It sounded like the Rat was going to act like nothing had happened between Libby Flanders and him. Was he that sure Melinda would never believe me if I told her what I saw?

Chad piped up just then and asked if Jeffrey was taking her to the barn dance on Saturday.

"Of course," Melinda said. She gave Chad a smile, just like a silly, naïve girl who had no idea she was being fooled.

I couldn't take it one minute longer. "Why doesn't anyone believe me?" I slammed my fork down. "Jeffrey Sullivan is a—"

"That will do, Andrea," Mother cut in. "Eat your supper without talking. Words are getting you into trouble this evening."

I clenched my jaw to keep from talking back and stared at my lap. If nobody believed me, then I would have to think of something drastic to get my sister out of this mess before she was humiliated in front of the entire town of Fresno—and us along with her.

Like a flash of lightning, an idea seared my mind. It was risky, and I had only one chance to make it work.

I hoped Melinda would forgive me.

Chapter 5

It was a lousy supper. I couldn't get away fast enough. Once Melinda started talking, she chattered on about "Jeffrey this . . ." and "Jeffrey that . . ."

She did it on purpose, I think, just to show she didn't believe me even a little bit. Or maybe she was trying to convince herself that I was wrong. Whatever the reason, I asked to be excused and ran up to my room to make plans.

During Melinda's jabbering, I learned that the Rat planned on picking her up for a buggy ride at two o'clock the next afternoon. I pulled out last year's copybook and scribbled a few notes. Then I spent the rest of the long evening avoiding my family.

That wasn't hard to do. It was warm—as usual during a

valley summer. The one place I knew nobody would come looking for me was up at my special spot.

So I went fishing. The creek usually runs low this time of year, but for some reason it wasn't the muddy trickle it had been last year. I baited my hook and tossed in my line. I didn't care if I caught anything or not. I wasn't fishing because I wanted to catch trout, but because I needed to think.

Fishing is good for thinking.

By the time the sun began to slip below the horizon, I knew what I was going to do. I rode home, rubbed Taffy down, and went to bed. I didn't sleep much.

The next morning I rushed through my chores and changed into riding clothes. The next step would be tricky. I had to get to town, but I didn't want anyone to know I was going.

"The things I do for my sister." I sighed and saddled Taffy. "If Mother catches me heading to town without permission, she'll skin me alive. Then she'll keep me busy doing extra chores for a month." I mounted and took off down the road.

By the time I trotted into Fresno, the sun was high overhead and blazing hot. "Now, where do you suppose the Flanders are staying?" I asked Taffy.

She shook her mane. I took a wild guess and figured they'd stay at the nicest hotel in town. That's where my family would stay.

"Whoa, Taffy." I pulled her to a halt in front of the Arlington Hotel. I slid from her back, wrapped the reins around the hitching post, and paused. "Andrea Carter, you are out of your mind," I told myself, gulping back my fear. Then I put one foot in front of the other and stepped up on the boardwalk.

The walk was not crowded. It was too hot for passersby to go strolling. I opened the door to the hotel and stepped inside. It was only a few degrees cooler in the lobby.

I almost turned tail and ran back outside. What if my plan

didn't work? What if Jeffrey was somehow able to sabotage my idea? He seemed determined to snag the girl of his choice—and leave two or three broken hearts strung out behind him.

Not if I can help it! I decided fiercely. The thought that my sister, whom I loved (even when she yelled at me and pretty much called me a liar) might get stuck with Jeffrey spurred me on. I approached the desk clerk and asked, "Are the Flanders staying here?"

The skinny, clean-shaven young man reminded me of Tim O'Neil, Justin's clerk. I could tell by the way he sniffed that he didn't really want to talk to me.

"Yes, miss," he finally said, frowning. "What is your business with them?"

I smiled and ignored his rude manner. "I wish to call on Liberty Flanders," I said politely. "Is she in?"

The clerk picked up a palm-sized silver tray and held it out. "Your card, if you please."

Calling cards. A waste of cards and the ink they're printed with. But for families as well to do and important as the Flanders (and the Carters, I reckon), name cards are the polite way of letting someone know you would like to call on them. Hence, a "calling" card.

I rolled my eyes and dug one of the pesky cards from my vest pocket. It was pale blue, with flowers scrolled around the edges. One line of script read "Andrea Rose Carter." I'd asked the printer for horses,  but alas, he didn't have any horses in his stock of movable type. He had flowers or birds or butterflies. Those were more ladylike anyway, he told me.

I dropped my card onto the tray.

The clerk glanced briefly at my card, and his eyebrows shot up. "I will return immediately, Miss Carter." He sounded friendlier this time around.

I watched him scurry up the stairs. "The Carter name is good for *something*," I muttered with a sense of satisfaction.

I expected to be invited up to the Flanders' hotel room, but the desk clerk returned with Libby at his heels. It was refreshing to see that she didn't take calling cards too seriously either.

"Andi!" Libby flashed me a friendly smile. She wasn't wearing her floppy hat, and she'd left her long hair down. Clearly, she was not expecting visitors.

"Howdy, Libby," I replied.

"I'm so glad you came by for a visit," Libby said. "The hotel room was getting quite crowded. I can't wait until the auction is over and we can do something more interesting while we're in town."

"Aren't you and Jeffrey Sullivan spending time together today?" I knew the answer, of course. The Rat was squiring Melinda around.

Libby's face fell. "He wanted to be with me, and we enjoyed breakfast together. But he had important business this afternoon that he simply could not put off. I felt so badly for him. He wanted to take me on a buggy ride out to the San Joaquin River. Maybe tomorrow."

My cheeks turned hot, and my heart raced. I wanted to blurt out to Libby what I'd told Melinda yesterday afternoon, that Jeffrey Sullivan was not who they thought he was. But I clamped my mouth shut. If my own sister didn't believe me, why should an acquaintance? Libby might think I was trying to break up her and Jeffrey.

This is getting complicated.

I moaned and shook my head. Then I sucked in a deep

breath and told Libby what I'd come to say in the first place. "I was wondering if you wanted to get out of town and go riding with me out on our ranch."

I sent up a quick prayer that she actually liked to ride and would want to go.

Libby's eyes sparkled. "Oh, Andi, I would!"

I suddenly wished Libby lived closer to Fresno. She was a lot older than I, but I could easily see us becoming friends. Then I sighed. After today, she would probably want to wring my neck for what I was about to do.

She would have to stand in line behind Melinda.

Chapter 6

This is for Melinda. This is for Melinda . . . and for Libby too.

I repeated it over and over as I waited for Libby to change into riding clothes and come back downstairs to the hotel lobby. Sweat trickled down the back of my neck, and not just because it was ninety degrees in the shade.

Not a great time of the day to go riding.

I had half expected Libby to put up some kind of protest. But she hadn't. She'd just skipped merrily back up the stairs and disappeared around a corner.

A new thought made sweat run down my neck even faster. What if Jeffrey canceled the buggy ride with Melinda? It was hot, and a buggy ride sounded dreadful. It was much better to at least feel some breeze on horseback.

I shook my head. No, the buggy cover was probably Jeffrey's way of showing off his new rig, and it would keep the sun off Melinda's face. At least, I *hoped* it was his way of showing off today. If for some reason he and Melinda decided it was too hot to go on a buggy ride, they would most likely stay indoors, chatting in the parlor.

The parlor. Not a good place to reveal my surprise. There are a lot of breakables in Mother's parlor.

I shook myself free of my gloomy thoughts and hoped things would play out like Melinda had so confidently announced at supper the night before.

"I'm ready," Libby said. She was dressed in riding clothes that made her look like the Queen of Hearts, all decked out in browns and creams, with a bright red blouse that matched the band around her straw hat.

"Father was glad to hear I'm going riding while he and Mother attend the auction. My choice was to accompany them or wait alone in our room. My sisters are already at a friend's home, where they'll stay much cooler. Father did wonder who was crazy enough to ride in the heat of the day." She giggled. "I guess *we* are. Thanks for your invitation."

"I'll go riding any time," I said, swallowing my guilt. Libby was so nice! She seemed ready to give anything a go, even sweltering under the August sun.

It took no time to grab Taffy and head for the livery, where Libby intended to rent a horse. She raved over Taffy then told me about her own mare back home, Cotton Candy, a pale cremello.

"We both named our horses after candy," Libby said with a laugh. "What does that tell you?"

"That we both like candy," I said, laughing with her. Inside I was not laughing. I was cringing. *I really like her!* I thought. *I hope she still likes me when this is over.*

Cory Blake readied Libby's horse for riding. He was all stares and questions while he saddled a sorrel gelding and led him outside. Then he helped Libby mount.

"Who's *she*?" he whispered just before I mounted Taffy.

"A new friend. I'm going to show her the ranch."

"In this heat?" Cory said in surprise. "You're *loco*."

Loco, *indeed!* I agreed silently. "I'll tell you all about it next week," I promised.

"So, there *is* a reason you're taking her riding during the hottest part of the day," Cory said. He smirked and slapped Taffy on the rump.

That Cory! He knows me too well. I gave him a warning look so he wouldn't let on to Libby that I was up to something.

He grinned, tipped his hat, and said, "You ladies have a nice ride now, ya hear?"

◆ ◆ ◆

It took longer than the usual hour to ride out to the ranch. I didn't want to take the main road, on account of maybe accidentally meeting Jeffrey on his way out there. I also didn't want to push the horses in this heat, especially Taffy. She wasn't due to drop her first foal for five more months, but I wanted to be careful.

I led Libby on the scenic route, through fields and past orchards, until we ended up on the far side of the Circle C. I pulled Taffy to a stop in a shady grove of oaks. It wasn't as hot as I feared. Today there was a breeze. Granted, it was a hot one, but a breeze is a breeze any way you look at it.

A few gulps from the canteen cooled my dry throat. Libby chugged down a good share of the canteen's contents as well. "Your ranch is beautiful," she remarked.

I followed her gaze to where the Sierras were peeking out above the rolling hills. I agreed wholeheartedly.

"We can see the mountains from the Triple L," Libby said, "but they don't look as stunning as they do from here."

In this part of the country, one ranch in the Sierra foothills looks just about like another, but it was sweet of Libby to compliment the Circle C. I looked up. The sun's position showed it was nearing two o'clock.

Now or never. My stomach churned as I nudged Taffy into a trot. "Come on, Libby. I'll show you the yard and the ranch house. Then I'll ask Nila for a tray of cookies and something cool to drink."

"Sounds lovely," Libby said. Sweat beaded her forehead and dripped freely down her face.

I turned Taffy toward the house and yard.

This is it.

Chapter 7

Libby stayed next to me as we made our way home. I knew it wasn't only the sun making my hands slick with sweat. I swallowed and tried to carry on a cheerful conversation.

Most days I wished the Rat would steer clear of our place. Not today. Today I hoped Jeffrey followed through on his promise to take Melinda buggy riding. This might be my only chance to show Melinda what lay behind Jeffrey's mask of affection.

With Libby here, I had a chance to prove I'd been telling my sister the truth.

We trotted into the yard. At first glance it looked deserted, and my heart fell to my toes. Then I spied the spanking-new buggy tied up under the shade of one of our giant oaks. The rig was a beauty, all right. I'd bet he waxed each spoke. His horse was a shiny bay, with every tangle combed out of its black mane and tail.

I dismounted and led Taffy to the watering trough. Libby followed me. She paid no attention to the buggy, which eased my momentary panic. What if Jeffrey had taken her for a ride already and she recognized the rig?

Apparently, Melinda was the first.

As the horses took their fill of water, I looked around for my brothers. I spotted Mitch ducking into the barn. He barely limped anymore. His shot-up leg had healed completely, but I still got shivers remembering our time up in the hills earlier in the summer.

Chad was nowhere in sight. He'd probably gone to the stockyards for the cattle auction. No matter. It was Melinda I wanted to find.

As if in answer to my wish, the front door of the ranch house opened, and Melinda stepped out onto the veranda. She was dressed up in a bright-yellow summer frock with a big, floppy sun hat.

Jeffrey Sullivan stood right behind her. His hands were wrapped around her face, covering her eyes. Melinda was giggling. He leaned close to her ear and mumbled something then guided her down the steps and toward the buggy.

Libby looked up from watering the horses. "Oh, there's your sister. It looks like she's going on a buggy—" She broke off and squinted against the sun. "Who is she with?"

The sun was pretty bright. If I hadn't known it was Jeffrey, I might have asked the same question. We were halfway across the yard, quite a distance from the veranda. But the Rat was wearing his signature top hat, the ugly thing. I would have recognized him anywhere.

I was glad Libby had not. My timing had to be perfect.

Jeffrey removed his hands from Melinda's eyes. She squealed with delight at the new rig. She threw her arms around Jeffrey's neck and looked up at him with adoring eyes. And then she let him *kiss her!* Right there in plain sight of the entire ranch. True, no cowhands were loafing, but the thought of it made me see red.

Caught up with each other, Jeffrey and Melinda paid no attention to Libby and me.

That was about to change.

Jeffrey escorted Melinda off the porch and helped her into the buggy. Talking and smiling, he circled around and took hold of the bay's bridle. Instead of climbing into the buggy beside her, he began to walk backward. He chatted with Melinda and led the horse toward Libby and me.

Jeffrey no doubt planned to give the horse a drink before setting out. If he knew Libby and I were there, I'm sure he would have taken off in the opposite direction.

Too late. Jeffrey wasn't watching where he was going. He kept walking backward, pulling the bay along and talking with Melinda. He didn't see Libby and me or our horses until he was practically on top of us. He bumped into the trough and let go of the bridle so his horse could drink.

"Howdy, Jeffrey," I said.

Jeffrey spun around . . . and froze.

Chapter 8

Up to that very second, Libby had not recognized Jeffrey, not with his back turned and never expecting to see him here with Melinda. But as soon as he twisted around, she knew him. Her eyes grew round as saucers. Two red spots flamed her cheeks. She gasped, and her hand flew to her mouth.

Jeffrey's expression told me everything. He knew that *I* knew he was a two-timing cheat who had just been caught with his hand in the cookie jar. His face turned the color of the chalk in my schoolroom. He didn't say a word, but his eyes shot daggers at me.

"I told you this wasn't over." I gave him my own icy-blue glare.

"What's wrong, Jeffrey?" Melinda called from the buggy. She couldn't see his face, but she could easily make out his stiff back and clenched fists.

"Ev . . . everything's all right," he said, clearing his throat. "Stay in the buggy, Melinda."

Melinda clearly had ideas of her own. She didn't like being bossed any more than I did. Instead of obeying the Rat, she climbed down from the rig. "What's wrong?" she asked Jeffrey again. She glanced at Libby then looked at me. "Andi, what are you up to?" She frowned in annoyance.

I opened my mouth to blurt the truth, but I didn't have time to say one word. Faster than a striking snake, Libby's hand reached out and slapped Jeffrey Sullivan across the face.

I gasped. Melinda gasped.

"How dare you!" That Flanders girl was smart as a whip. She'd figured everything out in the space of five seconds. "And to think I let you kiss me!"

Jeffrey stood stock-still. The handprint showed bright red against his pale cheek.

Melinda, who hadn't believed me when I told her about Jeffrey kissing Libby, looked at Libby with new eyes. She looked at me. Her face turned white. Then it turned red. "Do you mean . . ." She couldn't go on.

Libby was shaking in anger. "Andi, is this what you meant yesterday when you said Melinda would hear about this?"

By now, I'd recovered my wits. "Jeffrey's been courting her for over a year . . . or so he says. But it looks like he's trying to court *any* rich girl. Melinda didn't believe me, so I had to do something drastic to convince—"

I didn't get a chance to finish explaining. Jeffrey's hand curled around one of my braids, and he yanked me around to face him. His expression scared me. He looked meaner than a wolf stalking a lamb, and *I* was the lamb. He called me names that made Melinda and Libby squeal in astonishment.

Then Jeffrey began to drag me across the yard. "I'll teach you a lesson you'll never forget, you brat."

I kicked and hollered. With his free hand, Jeffrey smacked me on the face before other hands tore him away from me. I crumpled to the ground, breathing hard.

When I opened my eyes, I saw a sight that propelled me to my feet. Melinda and Libby—with Mitch's help—were hauling Jeffrey to the horse trough. Three heartbeats later, they shoved him in. The Rat kicked and splashed until I thought all the water would be thrown from the trough.

Mitch stood off to the side, arms crossed, and let the girls hold Jeffrey underwater. When Mitch saw me, he waved me over. I stumbled to his side. He put an arm around me and hugged me tight. "I heard the commotion and came as fast as I could," he said. "You all right?"

I nodded, but my face hurt. I reached up and felt my cheek. I winced. It was tender, but it wasn't bleeding.

"How long do you think they should hold him under?" Mitch asked. He was not smiling.

I shrugged and blinked back tears.

When the girls let go, Jeffrey erupted from the water like a geyser. Coughing, sputtering, and choking, he sat there trying to catch his breath.

Mitch reached down and yanked the half-drowned Rat out of the trough. Then he threw him to the ground. "Jeffrey Sullivan," he said, "your courtship of my sister is over. I'll inform my family. But just to be clear, if you ever come near either one of my sisters again, or this young lady"—he nodded at Libby—"you'll get more than a dunking from my brothers and me. Clear?"

Jeffrey sat there, chest heaving. Mitch knocked him over. "Answer me. Is that clear?"

Jeffrey nodded.

I shivered. Mitch looked scary-angry, not at all like the easy-going brother I knew and loved. But I was awfully glad it was Mitch and not Chad towering over this human mud pie. Chad might not have let Jeffrey come up for air, and I'd have to visit my brother in San Quentin penitentiary for drowning a man.

Mitch hauled Jeffrey to his feet then landed a sudden, swift blow to his jaw. Jeffrey went sprawling. He lay on the ground, clearly defeated, and made no move to rise.

"That's for touching my baby sister," Mitch said. He found Jeffrey's tall hat, filled it with water from the trough, and slammed it down on the Rat's head.

I was too astonished to cheer or do anything else. I glanced sideways at my sister. Melinda and Libby had their arms around each other. Both were sobbing.

When they saw me, Melinda opened her arms wide. "I'm so sorry I didn't believe you, Andi," she said, swiping at her tears. "Just look at you! You might end up with a black eye on account of all this." She sniffed. "Please forgive me."

I fell into Melinda's arms and started crying too. She hugged me. Then Libby hugged me.

"Thank you for caring enough to show us what kind of man Jeffrey Sullivan really is," Libby said.

I hugged Melinda and didn't let her go. Finally! Jeffrey Sullivan was banished from our lives.

Mitch strong-armed Jeffrey into his rig. "Take your buggy and get off our ranch." He slapped the horse on the rump to hurry him along. Then he winked at us girls and headed back to the barn.

"Thanks, Mitch!" I called.

"All in a day's work," I heard him say with a laugh.

About the Author

SUSAN K. MARLOW is a twenty-year homeschooling veteran and the author of the Circle C Adventures and Circle C Beginnings series. She believes the best part about writing historical adventure is tramping around the actual sites. Although Susan owns a real gold pan, it hasn't seen much action. Panning for gold is a *lot* of hard work. She prefers to combine her love of teaching and her passion for writing by leading writing workshops and speaking at young author events.

You can contact Susan at susankmarlow@kregel.com.